TIME OF MY LIFE

TIME OF MY LIFE

A Jazz Journey from London to New Orleans

CLIVE WILSON

With a foreword by Tom Sancton

UNIVERSITY PRESS OF MISSISSIPPI ✢ JACKSON

www.upress.state.ms.us

Designed by Peter D. Halverson

The University Press of Mississippi is a member of the
Association of University Presses.

Foreword © 2019 by Thomas A. Sancton

Portions of this work appeared in a different form in
New Orleans Music and *JazzBeat*.

"A Tale of Kid Howard" was originally published as a chapter entitled
"Kid Howard's Funeral" by Clive Wilson in *The Hottest Trumpet: The
Kid Howard Story* by Brian Harvey (New Orleans: Jazzology Press, 2007),
and is reprinted here by permission.

Appendix B: "What Does Louis Armstrong Mean?" was originally
published in *OffBeat* magazine, May 2001, www.OffBeat.com, and is
reprinted here by permission.

First printing 2019
∞

Library of Congress Cataloging-in-Publication Data

Names: Wilson, Clive (Trumpet player), author. | Sancton, Thomas (Thomas
Alexander), 1949–author of introduction.
Title: Time of my life : a jazz journey from London to New Orleans / Clive Wilson.
Description: Jackson : University Press of Mississippi, [2019] | Series: American
made music series | "First printing 2019." | "Portions of this work appeared in a
different form in New Orleans Music and JazzBeat." | "With a foreword by Tom
Sancton." | Includes bibliographical references and index. |
Identifiers: LCCN 2018032924 (print) | LCCN 2018038139 (ebook) |
ISBN 9781496821188 (epub single) | ISBN 9781496821195 (epub institutional) |
ISBN 9781496821201 (pdf single) | ISBN 9781496821218 (pdf institutional) |
ISBN 9781496821171 (cloth : alk. paper)
Subjects: LCSH: Wilson, Clive (Trumpet player) | Jazz musicians—United
States—Biography. | Jazz musicians—England—Biography. | Jazz—Louisiana—
New Orleans—History and criticism.
Classification: LCC ML419.W536 (ebook) | LCC ML419.W536 A3 2019 (print) |
DDC
781.65092 [B]—dc23
LC record available at https://lccn.loc.gov/2018032924

British Library Cataloging-in-Publication Data available

CONTENTS

FOREWORD

When Clive Wilson first showed up at Preservation Hall in 1964, I was a fifteen-year-old kid. Like Clive, I had fallen totally in love with the music of New Orleans. Unlike him, I was a native. Clive was one of the "jazz pilgrims"—young men (and a handful of women) who came from all around the world to learn at the feet of the city's aging black jazzmen. They came from England, Germany, Scandinavia, some from as far away as Japan. One of them, England's Sammy Rimington, had given me an old Albert system clarinet and started me on the road to becoming a musician myself.

I was fascinated by these visitors from across the sea. They were somewhat older than me, had exotic accents, came from parts of the world that I had never seen. They were enthusiastic, motivated, and almost worshipfully admiring of the local jazzmen they sought to learn from. They were there to soak up not just the sound of the music but the whole culture around it—the food, the parties, the parades, the ways of the old musicians who came from a world so different from their own. And to someone like me, who had grown up in the Jim Crow South, they were remarkable for their total lack of racial prejudice. For all those things, I admired these pilgrims and welcomed their presence—not least because they provided a cohort of young musicians with whom I could play in jam sessions at Preservation Hall and elsewhere. For whatever reason, I was the only one among my generation of local kids—white or black— who showed any interest in learning from the old masters. So the foreign visitors became my friends, my musical peers, and to some extent my role models.

Most of them stayed a few weeks or months and then returned home. After a short initial visit, Clive came back to the city and stayed. He not only stayed but became an important New Orleans musician himself. While learning his trade from the likes of Kid Howard, Alvin Alcorn, Percy Humphrey, and Dede Pierce, he began to play gigs in the French Quarter and elsewhere around town. After only a few years here, he landed in the trumpet chair of Papa French's Tuxedo Jazz Band, the successor to the legendary orchestra of Oscar "Papa" Celestin. He also plied the steamy back streets with Harold Dejan's Olympia Brass Band, where I would often find myself at his side "sitting in" with this famous marching group. At Mardi Gras, Clive would find himself on the music float of King Rex, or playing for some of the city's old-line Mardi Gras krewes. Along with other jazz pilgrims, he would show up at the backyard parties hosted by Kid Sheik Colar—jamming with the old-timers over beer, red beans, and crawfish—or Allan Jaffe's get-togethers in the rear courtyard of Preservation Hall, where my father first taught Clive how to eat boiled crabs.

But Clive wasn't there just to have a good time. He worked hard on his instrument, studied theory at Loyola University, took lessons with proper music professors. I was impressed by his work ethic on the trumpet and with his steady progress toward technical proficiency—all the while basing his playing on the spirit, emotional expression, and swing of the old New Orleans players. He truly became a New Orleans musician himself, one of the torch-bearing successors of the traditional style. Not the least of his contributions to the city's jazz culture were the recordings he produced on his New Orleans label, which featured historic performances by such legends as Jeanette Kimball, Herb Hall, Frog Joseph, and Dave "Fat Man" Williams.

I well remember the first time I saw Clive in the carriageway of Preservation Hall. He was holding his trumpet case and gazing at the band with a rapt expression. His blonde hair and youthful, almost juvenile countenance prompted my mother to say he looked like "a choirboy." Which is precisely what he had been back in England as the son of an Anglican vicar. And that is one of the most interesting things about his story: what drove an English public school boy, son of a clergyman, holder of a degree in physics, to cross the sea and embrace the music and culture of a band of aging black jazzmen? One can hardly imagine a wider cultural divide. This memoir explains the passion that led him to make that leap and not look back. In a way, it is the story of a young English adventurer who sails out to the colonies and "goes native." (Unlike Joseph Conrad's Kurtz, however, Clive preferred playing music to cutting off heads.)

Fortunately for us, Clive has been a keen observer as well as a participant in the New Orleans jazz scene. His dealings with some of the city's most interesting characters inspired the series of profiles that make them live and breathe on the page, with their voices, their humor, their musical ideas, and their philosophies about life. Among these close-up subjects are George Guesnon, Punch Miller, Alvin Alcorn, Emile Barnes, Harold Dejan, and the intriguingly eccentric Barbara Reid, the original founder of Preservation Hall.

This book is not simply the tale of a young English trumpeter who emigrates to New Orleans. Nor is it just about music. With Clive's own story as the central theme, it describes some important aspects of the city's history and culture in the latter part of the twentieth century. All the more reason to be glad that Clive Wilson came to our city, that he stayed, and that he has done so much to carry on our musical traditions.

TOM SANCTON

PREFACE

Looking back at my experience in the city of New Orleans, with her many interwoven and interlocking patterns of people, relationships, and music, gives me an insight I never had while I was immersed in it. This perception grows from the separation that comes with the passing of time and from the inevitable passing on of those whose home it was. New Orleans pulled me, a thread from a different cloth, slowly yet inevitably into her weave. Now, I can see how she drew me into her tapestry, how my thread became interwoven.

The separation made apparent the weave, the connection.

This memoir, with its many stories, describes how that tapestry grew without my conscious awareness. I needed to be open to receive what the city could teach, to be an apprentice not only to the musicians I encountered along the way but to something undefined that I can appreciate from this distance. My memories have arranged the reality of my past into a coherent pattern.

⚜

I wish to thank the following for their help and encouragement: Guido Cairo, Mike Casimir, Kelley Edmiston, Tom Jacobsen, Ken Pape, Paola Roncallo, Ray Smith, Paige Van Vorst, and the staff at the William Ransom Hogan Jazz Archive of Tulane University.

My thanks are due also to the editors and publishers of *New Orleans Music (incorporating Footnote)*, Terry Dash, Louis Lince,

Clive Wilson and Tom Sancton in New Orleans, 2010. Photo: Sylvain Sancton, used by permission.

and Doug Landau, for giving me permission to use material from articles I have written for that magazine.

My thanks to Lars Edegran of Jazzology Press for permission to reprint a chapter I wrote about Kid Howard in the book *The Hottest Trumpet: The Kid Howard Story*, and for excerpts from articles I wrote for *JazzBeat* of the GHB/Jazzology Foundation.

My thanks to Susan Tucker for her thematic insights and general advice, and for contributing the index to this book.

Special thanks go to Tom Sancton, author of his own memoir *Song for My Fathers*, for advice on memoir writing and for contributing the foreword to this book.

PROLOGUE

I am at a boarding school just south of London, where I have arrived only a few weeks before. I am thirteen. I walk into a common room at a mid-morning break. Our common room, with its green lockers lining the cream-colored walls, one for each of us boys, so boring and utilitarian, a cement floor, a billiard table, a table tennis table, is where we went between classes. There's a cheap record player. (Whose was it? Did it belong to us?) I hear an unusual sound; someone is playing music I'd never heard before. Drawn like a moth to a flame, I cross the room. The record jacket has a drawing in vivid color of someplace I'd never heard of in a place I'd never thought of: San Jacinto? How do you even pronounce it? New Orleans? Bunk Johnson? What a strange name. What sounds!

The instruments, weaving in and out of each other, form a tapestry of sound and rhythm that resonates with something within me, until now unknown, calling forth a range of feelings: strong and joyful, yet plaintive and poignant at the same time. I am not understanding it; I am not making any sense of what I am hearing. But in that moment, which remains with me today, making sense of my attraction is not important. Something stirs. The music has an intrinsic strength and power that I have not heard before and have rarely heard anything approaching it since.

It is "Tishomingo Blues," played by Bunk Johnson and his New Orleans Jazz Band.

His name, Willie "Bunk" Johnson, and the drawing of San Jacinto Hall in New Orleans on the record cover, is irresistible, conjuring up an image of another world; mysterious, unknown and enticing at the same time. Questions race through my mind:

What kind of music is this? Where is New Orleans? Who on earth is Bunk?

TIME OF MY LIFE

INTO THE UNKNOWN

The year was 1964, and I was twenty-one, soon to be twenty-two. The sign on the bulletin board read "Student North American Club," offering a chartered flight to New York and back—three months in the summer vacation—for £55. Amazing! Maybe I can go? A friend said: "Yes, it's a good deal. I went last year. You should go, why not?" Thinking fast; could I make it? I could visit New Orleans and try to get a job there to pay for the trip. I will have completed my physics degree course at Newcastle University, so why not? Then it all seemed to happen so suddenly, so quickly. The opportunity appeared, a door opening to a new world lying ahead. I knew that somehow I could do it but, as usual, my outward expression was calm and did not betray my inner excitement. I was used to going into the unknown and was never afraid to take a chance. My frequent hitchhiking up and down the A1 from Newcastle-Upon-Tyne in the North East of England to London and back had never been a problem, turning out to be a reliable form of travel. So what could possibly go wrong with a trip to States? I was in part naive, part devil-may-care, and part adventurous.

Making the arrangements began immediately. I asked a friend of the family who lived in San Francisco to sponsor me so I could get a "Green Card," the permanent resident visa, which would enable me to work. The interview at the US Embassy in London went smoothly—there were no restrictions or waiting lists in those days—and approval came a couple of months later. I had always taken jobs during university holidays to pay for my extra expenses, and now I was saving up for my trip. What a change this would be!

Although I grew up in London, my parents had recently moved to Church Stretton in Shropshire and, after many years in London, really enjoyed living in a small town in the country. Knowing I needed to save money for my trip, they helped by hiring me to clear some of their hugely overgrown and long-abandoned garden. The Long Mynd hills were right behind their house, and Wales was just a few more miles to the west. There was a golf course up and down the steep slopes of these hills that must have been the most strenuous in the world, and was great for tobogganing when it snowed in the winter. A steam traction engine rally was held in the fields around the town each year, and that was the first time I heard a steam-driven calliope. The sound echoed up and down the valley.

I don't remember how I got to London from Church Stretton, as we were not on any main road. But perhaps I had a ride to Shrewsbury—we were a mere thirteen miles to the south—and hitched to London from there. The wealthier class pronounced it SHROWsbury, but I never identified with them, so pronounced it SHREWsbury like the majority. Many of my new friends in the traditional jazz world of London, since we had only recently met, thought I came from Shropshire.

"You're getting away again," my sister Clare told me. My other sister Elizabeth had recently "got away" by taking a job as a secretary for the Royal Horticultural Society in Cambridge. That was arranged by my dad as she had been getting increasingly depressed living at home in London. My brother Mark was able to go to Cambridge too, following in his father's footsteps with a singing scholarship to Clare College, later studying divinity and becoming an ordained priest in the Church of England. My younger sister Clare was stuck at home longer, as she depended on our parents to help her through university. She took biology at London. I began finding ways to "get away" from home in my teenage years.

There was something liberating and, as you will read later, even necessary about getting away from home. Even my long bicycle trips exploring London were a big relief. Once, when I was eleven, I had an accident and suffered a concussion. It was my fault, but since then I have followed the rules of the road meticulously. My escape to the States, both from family and country, beckoned—an adventure, a path to follow. I simply jumped at the chance, just following my nose, as it were, knowing nothing of what lay ahead, but excited about the unknown, completely unaware of anything in my future that would result from my actions.

The chartered flight was the longest journey I had undertaken—about ten hours in those days including a refueling stop in Gander, Newfoundland. Having paid my transportation in advance—a Greyhound bus ticket cost ninety-nine dollars for ninety-nine days—I arrived in New York with only fifty dollars in my pocket. I was counting on getting a job to pay for the summer. By chance I recognized another student from university on the flight over who knew of some cheap addresses to stay in Manhattan. We ended up in a sort of hostel for homeless, runaway kids that was, in a way, kind of appropriate. Costing one dollar a night, it was on the Lower East Side. Knowing nothing about New York, that was quite accidental. But there I was in the old Russian and Ukrainian Jewish quarter, now also inhabited by the bohemian crowd who had recently moved over to escape the rising rents of Greenwich Village; it was a decidedly hip part of town.

My first impression of the States was of New York City—the noise, everything moving fast, the yellow cabs, hundreds of them, the almost continuous ambulance and police sirens, the energy. It was hot, dry, and dusty, yet the nights were comfortable. People were friendly. The very next day some of the bohemian types I met took me to the bar where the Beatles had spent a night and recommended many other things to do and see—like eating borscht in a Russian restaurant—that were unusual for me, coming as I did from a conservative British background. At night I heard the great trumpet player Henry "Red" Allen at the Metropole, and the New Orleans drummer Arthur "Zutty" Singleton at Jimmy Ryan's. As I could afford only one drink in each place, I would stand outside the Metropole, which was close to Times Square, and listen to several sets. The musicians would come out on the sidewalk to smoke a cigarette in their breaks. I plucked up enough courage to say hello to Mr. Allen, who seemed to tower above me, and told him I was on my way to his hometown New Orleans. His eyes lit up for a moment: "Have a good time," was all he said as he walked back to the bandstand.

After a few days I was riding the bus to San Francisco to visit my sponsor. You met all kinds on the bus so it, too, was an adventure. In fact, my first extended visit to the States was an adventure in trust. Everyone traveled by bus in those days except for the few who could afford to fly. I could get off and on wherever I liked, so took a route that passed by Flagstaff, Arizona, in order to visit the Grand Canyon. In those days Flagstaff was nothing but a little way station for visitors. It was a dry, semi-desert area surrounded by mountains covered in scrub. I tried to make the most of my one-day visit by walking halfway down into the canyon on a trail. That was a mistake as climbing back out was incredibly exhausting and took hours. Luckily there were water stations at regular intervals, but that was hardly sufficient. Hot, dusty, and dry, I climbed back into the bus to connect with the Greyhound bus which took me into San Francisco overnight. My arrival coincided with the Republican Convention, featuring the nomination of their candidate for president, a race between Goldwater and Rockefeller. As I got off the bus I found myself at the end of a demonstration against Goldwater and his public pronouncements on bombing Vietnam with nukes, if necessary. Goldwater won the nomination, but ultimately lost the presidential race to the Democrat candidate and incumbent president Lyndon B. Johnson, who had been Kennedy's vice-president.

My sponsor Norman Smith, an English friend of my family, had once been a curate training under my father in our Church of England parish. Having lived in Japan for many years, he loved the Japanese culture of San Francisco, and took me to a neighborhood restaurant where we were the only non-Japanese. He ordered everything in fluent Japanese. Ironically, he was off to Britain in a few days, so undertook to acquaint me with all his favorite haunts immediately. This included visiting the Episcopal cathedral, which I found to be decidedly opulent, largely due to the extravagant tastes of Bishop Pike—an eccentric, go-get-'em type. The bishop achieved some notoriety later when he wrote a book about looking beyond the grave for evidence of his son, who had committed suicide. After retiring, Bishop Pike began searching around Israel where his son had died, and eventually disappeared without a trace in the desert. When Norman drove me north to the California redwoods, everything seemed so different, so new, so vast, so exciting. The final year of my degree course had been grueling, and a complete change was just what I needed. But impatient to move on, I found myself once again on a three-day bus ride to the city of my dreams, New Orleans. At that time it never occurred to me to stay longer than the summer.

GROWING UP IN LONDON

For a long time, New Orleans had grown in my imagination. New Orleans jazz represented so much that I may never be able to put into words, but has fascinated me ever since I first heard that Bunk Johnson recording. A trumpet player who began playing at the turn of the twentieth century, Bunk was famous for his tone and inventive, rhythmic style. He recorded for the first time in the 1940s. Until then, I had never heard any jazz and almost no popular music of any kind.

The son of an Anglican clergyman, I grew up in St. John's Wood, a quiet residential area of northwest London, close to Regent's Park, Lord's Cricket Ground, and only two Underground stops to Baker Street. I walked to school and back, crossing Abbey Road by the EMI Studios where the Beatles later recorded. We lived in the vicarage next to the church on Hamilton Terrace, which was the widest residential street in London with a row of plane trees on either side. The grounds around the church and our garden were extensive, and part of my chores was to cut the grass each week in the spring and summer. It took two hours.

My father loved classical music and could have been a professional tenor. As he couldn't stand popular music and musicals, even his admiration for Paul Robeson was tempered by his dislike of his recording of "Ol' Man River." Be that as it may, I must have inherited my musical sense from my dad. He loved the sound of the trumpet, and I remember him playing me 78s of the Haydn

Bill Wilson, my dad, as I remember him, ca. 1959. Donated by
Margaret Wilson to the Clive Wilson collection.

trumpet concerto when I was quite small. My dad sang ecclesiasti-
cal tenor with the choir, and often with a professional quartet that
sang anthems for our Sunday morning service. He also sang solo
tenor in productions of the *Messiah* and the *Saint Matthew Passion*. He had so much volume when he sang in the congregation
that the rest of us in the family were a little embarrassed. I am the
oldest of four children with two sisters, Elizabeth and Clare, and a
brother Mark, who died in 2013. All of us took piano lessons for a
while and Mark also played flute and organ.

As I write this, a vague and rather odd memory comes back to
me:

I am playing a toy drum in a Christmas end-of-term show for
parents. I am five. Everyone in the class is playing a drum to
accompany our teacher at the piano. It sounds pretty chaotic as
no one else in the class can keep time including one boy who is

trying to conduct. I am so frustrated by this that I bang louder on my drum to try to get everyone together. So the teacher calls me up from the back row to take a turn conducting and I love it! But she doesn't like me, never did, and sends me to the back row again after one short piece.

My dad is quite excited to see me up there in front of everyone, the only one in kindergarten who can keep time. But he is pretty annoyed with the teacher. My mother is proud of me, but has a worried look on her face, that frown she often has. I imagine she thinks: No way! No drum set in our home! All that noise!

So that was the beginning and end of my drumming career.

As my first teacher disliked me, she made me feel pretty miserable at times. Maybe that had something to do with the ear infection I came down with that kept me out of school for many months. Although nothing seemed to work, it did eventually get better. I was kept back in the second year, because I had difficulty learning to read and do simple arithmetic. Eventually, the teacher in the third-year class (third grade) took a special interest in me and got me over the hump of learning the basics. However, I was eleven (in seventh grade) before I finally caught up with my own age group.

As for music, we had a school choir, but that was all. I was a member for a while because I could sing in tune. It was my dad's passion, so he was eager for me to pursue singing. At another school concert for parents when I was seven or eight years old, we sang the *Ave Maria*. I remember him feeling that was a mistake as he thought it too difficult for us at that age. He was a perfectionist. But later he told me we don't sing that in the Church of England because we don't worship the Virgin Mary like the Roman Catholics. That seemed a pity as I enjoyed the melody.

My dad had been a chorister as a boy. When his voice broke he stopped using it altogether for two years, even talked in whispers to protect it until it settled. He continued his training and won a singing scholarship to Clare College at Cambridge. After he decided to become a minister, singing took second place, but he remained a perfectionist whenever he performed music or church services. Unfortunately he and I had a problem. I wanted his approval, but he was not around that much. Nowadays I see him as a workaholic. I think he was avoiding closeness and felt uncomfortable with emotions. A product of his times at the beginning of the twentieth century, he believed in an old-fashioned way of bringing up kids, which I'm sure he had experienced himself. He didn't approve of too much holding and touching for boys. My mother later told me that when she was a young mother, she was quite influenced by this advice from both my father and her in-laws, and was often torn between that and following her own instincts. So, at least overtly, I didn't feel close to my dad. I felt a distance between him and myself, and I learned very early to do without his help. This was unusual, as most of my school friends liked to do things with their fathers.

We did *some* things together, of course. My dad played cricket and spent quite a bit of time giving me batting and bowling practice in the nets at Lord's Cricket Ground, which was just up the road from where we lived. He was a member of the Middlesex Cricket Club (MCC). But, unlike my brother, I didn't have the eye-to-ball coordination to become much good. Later, beginning when I was about eleven, he dug out all his old conjuring tricks and taught me to use them. My dad used to be a conjurer when he was in university. Although I loved working with the illusions, the sleight-of-hand tricks required considerably more practice and skill that I never mastered. Nevertheless, I put on a couple of successful shows at my primary school. I remember feeling both nervous and excited to perform in front of the other kids.

In my generation, families ate all their meals together, and conversations at the table could get quite lively. Once when I was eight and had just realized that Santa Claus was really my parents, I asked my dad how he could possibly believe in God when He was invisible. I was challenging him. "I don't see Him, so I don't believe He exists," I said. I must have hit a raw nerve: although it was very rare for my dad to show his anger—he avoided it if at all possible—he became infuriated with me for questioning the central fact of his life, his commitment to serving God, as he put it. His reaction was so unexpected that I went numb with shock and never dared to bring up that topic again. Today I wonder about that moment—his eldest son asking a philosophical question! He could have talked about Santa Claus, for example. Even though we cannot see him, the spirit of giving is nevertheless alive when we give gifts to each other at Christmas. Does God exist when we help others? I feel he missed a wonderful moment.

Like most children, I asked a lot of questions growing up but I could never get a straight answer from my dad. He fenced around the subjects, pretending to know so much, but never actually answering my question. Since he was brilliant at waffling around the topic and not coming to any definite opinion, I found him maddening and began to withdraw from him, keeping to myself. Sometimes I'd be so angry I'd stomp out and slam the door behind me.

Perhaps for that reason I did not relate to church. I never knew what to do there but sit it out. Growing up in a vicarage meant going to church on Sunday morning and Sunday school in the afternoon. On top of that, we read selected passages from the Bible at the breakfast table every day. I certainly became familiar with scripture. But enough was enough, so I said no when my dad asked me if I wanted to sing in the choir. That would have meant more choir practice and singing at more services, and I had quite enough church and religion to deal with as it was. A few years later I quit singing in the choir at school, probably because I associated it with church.

My mother was close to us because she was around all day long, except when we went to school. Her family meant everything to her and she had a hard time giving us up when we became old enough to move on. She would do *too* much sometimes. Helping me with my homework, she even wrote all my compositions for the English class until I was found out. I took an exam at eleven years old and could only write two lines. So they knew my mother had been doing it. But as soon as she stopped helping me, all of a sudden I could write about anything. It seemed I had picked up the ability from watching her.

At the same time that she had this desire to help us, she was the one who got angry. But she was unpredictable, which all of us found hard to deal with. Sometimes when we were naughty, she'd laugh it off. The next time she might explode with rage and banish us to our rooms until she had time to cool off. She also reacted if she thought there was any possibility of inappropriate sexuality, even at a young age when that was quite out of the question. For example, I remember feeling terrible shame one time when I was seven. I was playing children's games with a new friend I had met on holiday and put my arm around her. My mother walked in the room and went through the roof! And there were other occasions. It was a sensitive issue.

For some reason, my mother thought all men were untrustworthy except her father, and all women were good except her mother. That left a kind of unacknowledged cloud hanging over us at home, a cloud that I had no way of verbalizing when I was young. I was so used to this atmosphere that I only noticed it when I was nine and began to stay with another family from time to time. They had a small farm in Chesham, just outside London, with a variety of animals to feed, a pony to ride, and a model railway. I had so much fun there; it felt so liberating. And part of the excitement was that to get to Chesham from the Metropolitan Line, you had to change to a side line, a train that was pulled by a steam engine. Life was very different outside my home, so I know it wasn't because of the times we lived in. Looking back, I believe that was when I began to withdraw from my family. Of course, there were many advantages to living in London. Theater in the West End was cheap if you sat in the "gods," as the upper circle was called, and I was able to see several plays that we were studying in school performed by the Royal Shakespeare Company for almost nothing. Our church also sponsored a youth club which met once a week in the basement of a nearby Baptist church. We had the use of gym equipment, table tennis, and more. As boys, we were discovering girls, and the girls were discovering boys. It was a fun night out, and some of the friends I made then are still friends.

Today I am certain my mother was afraid of something, and afraid of letting my dad spend time with his children unless she was present also. Perhaps she was jealous of our affection for him, or his affection for us? At the same time, she worked tirelessly—all the chores, which we learned to help with, as well as taking on a lot of unpaid parish work. She was brilliant at cooking up meals on an almost zero budget, catering a reception, organizing events, and being the perfect hostess. And she encouraged me with the piano lessons that I began at age seven. I enjoyed piano even though I found it difficult. Simply put, it wasn't my instrument and I gave up trying when I was twelve. My mother was very upset with me for that, as I imagine she could sense the musician in me. But at the time I was very involved in the academic requirements of the entrance exams for my next school. We were under a lot of pressure.

But it was in my next school that I heard jazz for the first time.

FIRST EXPOSURE

Traditional jazz was popular in Britain and all over Europe. Quite the craze for some years, a couple of songs actually made it to the Hit Parade—*Petite Fleur* played by Monty Sunshine with Chris Barber's band, and *Samantha* and *Midnight in Moscow* played by Kenny Ball. Humphrey Lyttleton's *Bad Penny Blues* and Acker Bilk's *Stranger on the Shore* were big hits, too. So there were many of us teenagers who were falling for this new sound, especially the recordings of New Orleans musicians such as George Lewis, Kid Ory, and Louis Armstrong. I began to collect a few records with my meager allowance, and by the time I was sixteen we had quite a variety between us at school. So, learning that the Lewis band were going to tour Britain that winter, we decided to go and hear them. An "old boy" from the school offered to drive four of us up to the New Victoria Theatre in London. Getting permission from my housemaster actually turned out to be easy enough when I told him that the band played "classical" jazz. In his mind, I was a student of some serious form of music as yet unknown to him.

The performance by George Lewis and his lively band from New Orleans was the first time I heard live jazz. Britain's Ken Colyer's Jazzmen played the warm-up set and, with the exception of Colin Bowden at the drums, who was clearly enjoying himself, they played their music with a humble sincerity and seriousness. After a short intermission, the Lewis band took over and it was immediately obvious that something had been missing with the

British band. With Lewis on the clarinet, Avery "Kid" Howard on trumpet, Jim Robinson on trombone, Joe Robichaux at the piano, Alcide "Slow Drag" Pavageau on bass, and Joe Watkins at the drums, the music just flew out of them with a joyful abandonment. I was familiar with some of their recordings, but hearing them and seeing them in the flesh was an ecstatic experience. They had so much spirit and spontaneity, joy and exuberance, which was in complete contrast to normal British behavior and the reserved way the Ken Colyer band presented themselves. Though diminutive and slim, George Lewis played with a sound that seemed to sing straight from his heart. And Kid Howard, short and round, played with an urgency and drive. By contrast in appearance, the exuberant Jim Robinson was tall and gangly with round, high cheekbones like a Native American. He bounced around the stage constantly, sliding his trombone from one note to the other for the sheer joy of it. A sublime glow lit up Slow Drag's face as he and Joe Watkins drove the band from one climax to the next. The audience went wild when Robichaux turned and sat down on the piano keys to imitate the tiger's roar in *Tiger Rag*. Those were the days when a New Orleans band could draw six thousand fans in England, and they would give them a tumultuous reception.

Everything about them was so rhythmic, even the way they moved on stage—like a dance, a dance between the different instruments, and a dance between them and us, the audience. We could have been in a sanctified church. A friend of mine once said that musicians were divided into two types—those that love the George Lewis band, and those that didn't realize they could blow them off the stage at any time!

Visiting New Orleans was quite out of the question, however. I was only sixteen, and travel of any kind was way beyond my means. I suppose I must have dreamed of the possibility. But I had a problem, which is laughable now that I think of it: I thought I'd never be able to eat the food. New Orleans musicians were always talking about red beans and rice, and I couldn't stand rice. I had

The George Lewis Band, mid-fifties: Alton Purnell, p; Kid Howard, tp; Lawrence Marrero, bj; Jim Robinson, tb; Slow Drag Pavageau, b; George Lewis, cl; and Joe Watkins, d. Photo: Courtesy of the Al and Doris Kershaw Collection, Hogan Jazz Archive, Tulane University.

only eaten it as rice pudding, sweet rice, which made me want to gag—still does. As we always ate potatoes in those days, I had not discovered that I would love savory rice. A couple of years later when I began to eat rice with Chinese food and Indian curries, I was so relieved. New Orleans became a possibility after all.

Although smitten by New Orleans jazz, I listened to a variety of styles as several of my friends at school were collecting records too—British bands like Ken Colyer, Humphrey Lyttleton, and Chris Barber, American jazz from Lu Watters to Louis Armstrong, and the occasional swing band such as Lionel Hampton, Benny Goodman, and Count Basie. Jimmie Rushing, Basie's singer, was one of my favorites.

But I could tell the difference very early on between the New Orleans musicians and traditional jazz players from elsewhere.

New Orleans musicians played with a greater depth of feeling without relying on fast tempos or flashy technique, perhaps expressing their experiences of life directly, yet with an irrepressible natural buoyancy and joy. "Trad" jazz, as we called it, though very popular in Britain and Europe during the 1950s and early 1960s, developed in a different environment for a different audience, never attaining the same emotional depth. But the best part about it was that everyone danced to it, and this may be the number one reason it became so popular. We danced the "jive," derived from the jitterbug, which was brought over to Britain during World War II by the American soldiers. The spin-off was an interest in New Orleans and a market for recordings by American bands. So besides the British bands, I became very familiar with the New Orleans jazz pioneers such as Johnny Dodds, "Jelly Roll" Morton, and Edward "Kid" Ory.

Kid Ory, the great New Orleans trombonist and bandleader! That's who I was lucky enough to hear next, one year after hearing George Lewis. We got permission from boarding school to go up to London once again. Another wonderful experience, it was also the first time I heard Red Allen, a great trumpet player from New Orleans. He was too advanced for my taste at that time, but I knew he was important. What really sticks out in my memory is the full-throated roar of Kid Ory's trombone completely filling the auditorium as the curtain went up. It must have been the trombone break at the beginning of "Original Dixieland One-Step." It sent chills down my spine. The power behind those musicians was stunning.

By this time I just had to find a way to listen to more bands and soak up as much as I could. Amateur bands were playing in pubs all over Britain, including one every Friday night in Ashstead, a neighboring village a mile or so away from school. I used to sneak out on my bike at night during "prep" time to go hear them. I'd have got into serious trouble if I'd been found out, but never was. One time, caught in the rain on my way back to school and soaked to the skin, I crept in the back way and rushed down to the changing rooms to get out of my wet clothes before anyone noticed. I also heard Acker Bilk and several other professional bands, either at dances or at jazz festivals. On school holidays, I began going to the 100 Club and Ken Colyer's Club in London. I even tried to dance. I felt free. Life at home felt cramped. A jazz club added a new dimension, like a breath of fresh air. There was a whole world beyond home and school out there waiting for me.

FIRST TRUMPET

I am with my family at a country fete, probably a church fair. It is late afternoon and we are getting ready to leave when a bugler stands up and begins playing taps. I stop, fascinated. How does he make a sound by blowing into that thing? My family has moved on and I am holding them up. But I cannot leave. My mother calls to me and finally comes over, takes my hand and drags me away. "We must go," she says. Perhaps she is worried about the noise I would make if I had a bugle of my own. I am eleven.

So things had to wait until I was in boarding school away from home and became eligible for the drum and bugle corps. I was sixteen. Self-taught bugler I quickly became, swollen lips and all, and following the example of a friend, found a secondhand cornet at a junk shop in Kingston-on-Thames for five pounds.

There were others in school also interested in playing jazz. Chris Jackman played the piano and Chris Watts the trombone. Later, we had Fred Ranger on piano, Rickie Gray on guitar, Chris Williams on clarinet, Mike Colvin on drums, and Nick Rowling on a tub bass. We formed a band and began learning tunes. The first tune I learnt was the spiritual "Sing On" from a Chris Barber recording, followed by "The Saints," of course. By the end of that year we managed to get through a few tunes at our yearly glee club concert. This was when anyone could get up and sing or play pop music, folk music, or rock 'n' roll. We closed the concert and were a sensation. It was my first experience of playing to an audience

School jazz band hamming it up, 1961. Rickie Gray, g; Nick Rowling, b; Chris Williams, cl; Chris Watts, tb; Clive Wilson, tp; Mike Colvin, d; Fred Ranger, p. Photo gifted by Chris Watts to the Clive Wilson collection.

and we had to play an encore. Surprised and elated, I was hooked on the applause and the approval I felt.

Apart from piano, music was not taught in my school. The piano teacher also played the organ in our school chapel. Self-taught on the cornet at first, I mistakenly thought that was important, just to play by ear. Although I could read a little from my piano lessons, I was not a sight-reader. Many of the New Orleans musicians I later met would laughingly say: "I don't read, but I can spell pretty good!" So I guess I could spell, but had no technique and little knowledge of music.

However, something prompted me to take lessons from the cornet player Owen Bryce when I saw his ad in *Melody Maker*, the popular music weekly in Britain. This was my own idea. I needed to be independent from my father and my family. The lessons with Owen were a revelation; he showed me how to begin using scales and broken chords or arpeggios, to begin to embellish the melody using the notes of the chords, and what to practice to become familiar with them. Though this was elementary, I knew almost nothing about music until then. I'll say this for Owen, he was very fussy about playing in tune, and trumpets are slightly out-of-tune instruments. He was never satisfied until I lipped the notes into the correct pitch—a good habit to pick up and essential ear training.

A year or so later, I began to be dissatisfied with imitating British trumpet players like Ken Colyer and Ken Sims, who was Acker Bilk's trumpet player.

"But I don't want to sound like an English trumpet player," I told Owen. "How can I sound like a New Orleans trumpet player?"

"Well if you want to sound like an English trumpet player, listen to English trumpet players. And if you want to sound like a New Orleans trumpet player, you should listen to New Orleans trumpet players!"

This seemed obvious advice, even a kind of permission to move away from being English. I started listening exclusively to New Orleans trumpet players like Bunk Johnson, Kid Howard (whom I associated with George Lewis), and Thomas "Mutt" Carey (who had played with Kid Ory). Many others were to follow as I became familiar with more recordings.

My parents had mixed feelings about my new interest in playing jazz, at least initially. My mother continued to get upset at the sound of me practicing, even when I used a mute. "Stop that!" she'd say. "I'm trying to put the little ones to bed." It was depressing. But they both liked the idea that this was making me happy. So my dad arranged with my Uncle Joe to buy me a secondhand trumpet for ten pounds. That doesn't sound like a lot, but it was the equivalent to about two hundred dollars today. My parents could not afford that. Although we had a big house to live in provided by the parish, my dad was poorly paid. With the expenses of rearing four children and sending them to school, there was nothing left over. We had very few toys and often made our own playthings. Later

I found out we had been overdrawn at the bank by an average of £500 (half my dad's yearly salary) for at least fifteen years and my parents were understandably stressed about it. But my godfather Uncle Joe was a surgeon, and gladly paid for my first trumpet. So in spite of my need to do my own thing my way, I was getting support when I most needed it.

SCHOOL

Playing music as a profession never entered my head. I felt that playing the trumpet would be a great hobby, that I would enjoy playing jazz as an amateur, for I had the idea to be a scientist of some description. Although I thought I was independent, actually I was following along a path that was expected of me; that is, no other alternative occurred to me. I was a product of my environment, my conditioning, if you will. It was primary school until thirteen, boarding school until eighteen, university for three or four years, and get a job—passing exams along the way to get from one to the next. I had to decide by the time I was fourteen whether to eventually specialize in science or languages. I had shown promise in writing; the school recommended I focus on English literature and languages, and they may have been right. But I chose differently once again. I insisted on science. I did well enough academically to take physics at Newcastle University. It was a tough course and I was committed to getting my degree. But I soon found myself spending a little of my time listening to local bands and badgering them to let me sit in. I was such a beginner this was not always popular. Incidentally, we used to hire a local rhythm 'n' blues group for our university hops called the Alan Price Combo that featured Eric Burdon on vocals. They played Joe Turner/Pete Johnson tunes at that time. But soon they became stronger than the Rolling Stones. I heard both groups in club dates and dances. The Alan Price Combo eventually turned professional and changed their name to the Animals.

Thanks to the Jazz at the Philharmonic concert series that came to Newcastle, I heard a variety of jazz musicians, including Errol Garner, Dizzy Gillespie, Oscar Peterson, Roy Eldridge, and Coleman Hawkins. Then there were blues singers who toured in Britain as well—Chris Barber and some of the British blues bands would book them—men like Sonny Terry and Brownie McGee, Howling Wolf, and Champion Jack Dupree. I liked it all except John Coltrane and Eric Dolphy, whose avant garde music gave me a headache. But they were such great musicians, and all the more reason why I thought of myself as an amateur, a real beginner. The concert that most impressed me, however, was Mahalia Jackson at the Royal Albert Hall in London. She was touring with her pianist Mildred Falls, just the two of them, and the concert was a sell-out! I'll never forget her. I had chills going down my spine for two whole hours. At the time I had no idea she was born in New Orleans.

I worked hard, but the physics course was an uphill struggle. Some of the students found it less hard. That was the difference. They really were scientists at heart. By contrast, I was finding out that my passion was New Orleans jazz. And incidentally, I had no idea what a young man with a physics degree could do for a living. During all my years of education, no one ever mentioned the type of employment that was possible in physics. So not knowing what my future looked like, I applied for a teacher training course after my bachelor degree in order to have a day job that would enable me to play music on the side.

Although I was slowly becoming aware of the importance of jazz in my life, that was not the only developing area. My thinking on many matters evolved. In my boarding school years, for example, I began by believing in the British private school system (called public schools in Britain) without realizing that it fostered a sense of superiority and unquestioning allegiance to the hierarchy that runs the country. This kind of allegiance is essential if you want to succeed in the civil service, the armed forces, or indeed any large corporation. On top of that, it was an all-male environment. The only contact we had with the opposite sex was with the matron in the infirmary, quite a personality. With her ample figure, we thought she looked like a ship in full sail as she strode across the quadrangle in her white uniform! As a result, my own sisters were comparative strangers to me when I went home in the vacations, and that is one of my big regrets. Girls were the great unknown, although I certainly found them attractive. And when I began to mix and go out with girls at university, ordinary friendship was difficult for me and I always ran from intimacy. I had no experience of them as people. I blame the segregated boarding school for that. Probably around sixteen or seventeen years old, I began to disapprove of the system, finding it anachronistic, reminiscent of the belief in the British as God's chosen people and England as the New Jerusalem. That might sound like I'm exaggerating, but I can assure you I heard some people express those sentiments!

I felt the same way about the kind of religion we were fed. I sat through a few "hell-fire and brimstone" sermons at school— though I must say that even the headmaster objected to that, and the school chaplain was asked to resign. Although my dad never preached that way, I had a lingering dread of ending up on the outside of heaven if I didn't go to church on Sunday—a fear that gradually dissipated during my late teenage years.

So I began to feel I didn't fit in with the boarding school system, but there was no way I could express my feelings about it openly without becoming an outcast. I was increasingly depressed. But listening to jazz, playing the trumpet, and breaking school rules by going to a pub on the weekends lifted my spirits. My mood depended on what I was doing. Depression is a bit of an extreme word perhaps, but I *did* feel melancholy. It began when I felt let down by my parents, when I began to see they didn't always live up to the ideals they professed. Looking back now, I can see I was increasingly unhappy at home. I did not have a sense of belonging there. But where in the world *would* I belong? My future was a complete unknown. Hiding my true feelings away, I learned to

SCHOOL27

adapt to my parents and my home environment. I was a very serious young boy much of the time, and so it is not surprising that my
parents were pleased that New Orleans jazz made me happy.

Of course, going to boarding school was another escape from
my environment at home, and although I felt abandoned and cried
on my first day there, a part of me welcomed the change. The key
to survival at a British public school is learning to fit in, to be part
of the crowd, and not to make enemies. The whole school ran hi-
erarchically, really a disguised bully system, although it was not
as tough as it had once been some years before my time. Those
above—more senior—command those below, a mind training system masquerading as character development: you do what you're
told or else. Academic achievement was all very well, but those
who were naturally good at sports tended to be more popular and
more valued. Feeling somewhat sidelined and overlooked, I had
the impression that those who were good at sports were thought
to have greater character development, greater team spirit. That
only changed when I ran unexpectedly well for my team in a
long-distance cross-country race, and the same year began playing
the trumpet in our school jazz band.

So I suppose the need to adapt to my surroundings has been
both a problem and a benefit. A problem in that I was not myself,
and not really happy about who I had become in order to survive,
and a benefit in that I enjoyed fitting in with people from different countries or backgrounds—in fact, anyone outside the home
and school environments I grew up in. Getting away from home
and doing my own thing like playing jazz made me happy. Experiencing different societies and cultures without judgment made me
happy.

I began to question my family's beliefs and customs, at first just
organized religious dogma and all-male boarding schools. But
once in university, out of the protected, somewhat cloistered environment of home and school, I became interested in so much
more: in psychology, from Wilhelm Reich to Carl Jung; in the

new wave of cinema, from Jean Cocteau to Fellini; and in social reform, nonviolent direct action as practiced by Gandhi, Martin Luther King and the Ban-the-Bomb movement. For a time, naively, I thought we might be able to change the world. I followed all the news of the civil rights movement in the United States, which actually *was* producing change and brought about the passage of the Civil Rights Act on July 4, 1964, coincidentally just a few days before my first visit.

On top of that, I was meeting other musicians in London on my vacations between university terms. Joining in with an amateur pick-up brass band on the annual Ban-the-Bomb marches, which took place every Easter, we attempted to play in the New Orleans parade style. I remember playing from Knightsbridge to Trafalgar Square on the last day of the march, when the numbers swelled to hundreds of thousands. I did this for several years until the marches ended when Kennedy and Khrushchev signed a treaty banning atmospheric testing. Perhaps we had *some* influence after all?

The march also reunited me with several friends from those days in London before I went to boarding school. Besides Sunday School, we had a lot of fun together on the youth club evenings. Although many of the parents despaired of their kids and thought they would never amount to anything, Robin Harper became the first Green Party member of the Scottish Parliament, Alan Crisp worked his way up to Harvard Business School and today runs his own successful company, Ewan Harper became the senior pilot with British Midland Airways, and Philip Stevens became one of the leading restorers in the world of Old Master paintings and manuscripts. None of them knew what he would become in life, yet each one of them succeeded by following a dream. My dream, though unformed, vague and distant from my consciousness, nevertheless drew me inexorably along its own path.

Through playing in the Ban-the-Bomb march, I met many others who knew a lot more about New Orleans than I—people like trumpeter Dan Pawson, trombonist Mike Casimir, banjoist Ashley

Keating, trumpeter B. Minter, and the Australian clarinetist Nick Polites. In fact, Nick's band was the first one I sat in with at Ken Colyer's Club in London, in 1963. When Ashley told me he had come through New Orleans on his way over to Britain from Australia, I resolved then and there to visit the city myself as soon as possible. One thing led to another, and the next year, Sammy Rimington, who had joined Ken Colyer's band playing the clarinet very much in the style of George Lewis, encouraged me to sit in with them. They were considered the preeminent New Orleans style band at that time. Colyer used to say "OK for three tunes" so he could go off and have a drink. One time, I remember missing quite a few notes with Bill Colyer, Ken's brother, sitting in front of me shaking his head. After one of those nights—it was a New Year's Eve—we took a crazy drive around a packed Trafalgar Square in Sammy's little two-seater sports car with his new wife Nina in the front. Four of us sat on the trunk, hanging on for dear life. That's how I first met Nina Rimington (now Nina Buck), who today runs her own club and restaurant in the French Quarter of New Orleans, the Palm Court Jazz Café.

Gradually, I was learning many more tunes from recent recordings in New Orleans that were coming out on the Riverside, Atlantic, and Icon labels, but my knowledge was very limited. At Dobell's Record Shop in the West End of London I could listen to records in a booth before buying them. I noticed a jump in a George Lewis recording of "Just a Closer Walk with Thee." "George Lewis *jumps* and you're complaining!" they exclaimed when I took the record back, much to the amusement of the other customers within earshot. Doug Dobell kindly explained to me it was actually in the recording itself. The bass player, Chester Zardis, was jumping up and down with so much enthusiasm while playing that the cutting needle bounced off the master in one spot.

My lack of familiarity with the old pop songs that were the standard fare in the repertoire was a major difficulty, so I had to learn them one at a time from recordings. Like many others, I was memorizing the way the tunes were played by imitating the record-ings. And I felt pretty good trying to play like a New Orleans trum-pet player; at least it was fun to have that fantasy. Copying from records is a start, but without technique, not much of a tone, and a limited sense of rhythm, I had little success. I played the trumpet incorrectly, blowing my cheeks out and using a lot of pressure. So I didn't sound like the guys on the records even though I was trying to mimic some of their phrases. I look at it like this: I was learning a new language, but I was on the outside of the music looking in. The more experienced musicians were very helpful and generous, however, introducing me to recordings I was unaware of, such as those on Bill Russell's American Music label that were first issued in the 1940s, where I heard trumpet players with exotic names like "Wooden Joe" and "Kid Shots" for the first time.

When my parents moved out of London to Shropshire, I was always made welcome to stay at either Ashley Keating's or Mike and Valli Casimir's flat in West London. All my new friends loved New Orleans jazz, and several of them had made the trip—Sammy Rimington and Mike Casimir among them.

"It's fabulous, fabulous. You must go!" exclaimed Sammy.

Ashley and Mike gave me the names of several people in New Orleans who could be helpful, and when Mike drove me to the airport, his parting words were: "Have a good time, and listen to it all."

Many years later, I discovered that my parents had sent Mike and Valli flowers with the note attached: "Thank you for making Clive happy."

CITY OF DREAMS

By taking temporary jobs in the university breaks, I had been saving up for my trip. I scraped together enough for the student charter flight—£55 round trip to New York (the rate of exchange was $2.80 to the pound back then)—applied for my green card, took my finals in the summer, and flew off to the States in July. I had three months, and I was counting on getting a temporary job in New Orleans to pay for it. But by the time I was ready to leave San Francisco, I had almost run out of money and borrowed another fifty dollars from my sponsor.

When I arrived in the late afternoon at the Greyhound bus station, blinded by the sunlight reflecting off the white concrete outside, the blazing heat and humid air made me feel like I had walked into a steam room. I overheard two older white men arguing: "Now tell me this," said the one doing the talking. "What *I* did *you* that made *you* do that to *me*?!" I had to wonder—what kind of parallel universe was this?

There was a choice of youth hostels to stay at, either three dollars a night or one dollar a night. I chose the cheaper one, only to find it was the "colored" youth hostel, which was more of a shelter on Dryades Street in Central City for the homeless and down-and-outs. Although segregation did not disappear overnight, these considerations never occurred to me. However, it was cool, nobody bothered me, and I think they were quite amused by my presence. I stayed a couple of nights.

Having made several friends on the bus ride—with three days in the same small space, you get to talk to everyone—we agreed to meet up in the French Quarter that evening. We strolled up and down Bourbon Street, and I noticed that the once lively El Morocco was nothing but an empty barroom, and the Mardi Gras Lounge, still owned by clarinetist Sid Davilla, had become a strip joint. We passed by Al Hirt's and Pete Fountain's clubs, listened to a little of the music outside the Paddock and the Famous Door, then wandered into the Absinthe House to hear Narvin Kimball and the Gentlemen of Jazz.[1] There was a dance floor in front of the band, but the club was nearly empty. Kimball came over to our table to ask if we would like to hear anything special, and all I could think of at that moment was a song recorded by Kid Sheik in Britain—"When Your Hair Has Turned to Silver." White-haired Narvin looked at me in a funny kind of way, but played it just the same.

The next day I explored the French Quarter, and found Dixieland Hall on Bourbon Street and Preservation Hall on St. Peter Street around the corner from a dismal Chinese grocery that later became the Maison Bourbon. Both venues must have seemed an enigma to the Bourbon Street club owners, since neither had a liquor license, preferring the radical approach of charging a mere dollar per person at the door, collected in a kitty basket.

I went straight to Preservation Hall that night. Two old instrument cases hung one above the other over the sidewalk. The top case, made for a trombone, was long enough for PRESERVATION to be lettered across it; the smaller clarinet case beneath spelled HALL. Peering through the windows of the French doors that used to open onto the sidewalk, the glass smeared and yellowed with age, I could make out the backs of the musicians blowing inside, with people sitting on rough benches, secondhand church pews, and old cushions on the floor. An iron gate to the side of this stuccoed wood-frame building led into an ancient-looking carriageway running alongside the converted rooms where the musicians played. Another gate further back opened onto a patio where I could make out cracked pavement, a small fountain, banana trees, and a side building with an overhanging gallery that used to be servants' quarters above, and stables below for the horses that pulled the family's carriage when it had been a private residence. The original creaky wooden floor remained and the walls were covered with oil paintings of many of the musicians. A huge exhaust fan in the back attempted to keep the place cool, but to no avail. It was hot. Yet Jim Robinson's band—which included several musicians I'd heard in London with George Lewis five years before: drummer Joe Watkins, bassist "Slow Drag" Pavageau, and pianist Joe Robichaux—was playing with great spirit and gusto. Now, instead of hearing them in an auditorium, I was just a few feet away, sitting on one of those cushions on the floor right in front of the band. This informality, this intimacy, this closeness between the musicians and myself was a completely fresh experience and had such an impact. Their music throbbed with life, with exuberance, with fun, and with a rocking rhythm I had never known before.

Looking back, I must have had a lot of faith arriving in the States with only fifty dollars in my pocket. That was all I could borrow and scrape together after paying for the student charter flight and the Greyhound bus ticket. As it turned out, there was nothing to worry about as everyone I met seemed to know everyone else, and either suggested a cheap place to stay—a Mrs. Noone's at 931 Chartres Street where the rent was twelve dollars a week—or knew someone who could give me a job to pay for my trip. From Jerry Cushman at the New Orleans Public Library, to Allan and Sandra Jaffe at Preservation Hall, to Dick Allen, Paul Crawford, and Betty Rankin (a.k.a. Big Mama) in the Archive of Traditional Jazz at Tulane University, and to the writer Tom Sancton, whose teenage son Tommy was learning to play the clarinet from none other than George Lewis, the overwhelming feeling I received was one of welcome: we share a common love for this music we call New Orleans jazz.

726 St. Peter Street (now Preservation Hall) in the 1920s. Photo: Barbara Reid collection, gifted by Kelley Edmiston (daughter of Barbara Reid) to the Clive Wilson collection.

"Come over on Sunday afternoon," said Jaffe one day. "I'll get Punch Miller and Eddie Summers and Tommy. We'll have a jam session and Punch can give y'all a lesson. If we each put up a little money; that will help him out." And so it became a quite regular Sunday event.

Imagine—lessons with the legendary Ernest "Punch" Miller, the trumpet player who made such great records in the 1920s up in Chicago! Afterward, we sat around in the courtyard behind the Hall with a sack of boiled crabs. Tommy's father showed me how to open them.

Within a week it seemed I had made a hundred new friends. It was a fabulous place in which to find oneself . . . or lose oneself. Was I dreaming?

A TALE OF PUNCH MILLER

The once-great trumpet player Punch Miller had come home in the mid-1950s to retire from his life as a traveling musician and spend his last days in New Orleans. But several people who knew of his long career, Larry Borenstein among them, had other ideas. Larry, who had an art gallery on St. Peter Street next to the famous bar Pat O'Brien's, decided he wanted to hear this man play again, and invited him and some other African American musicians he knew to come over and play a jam session. Punch was glad of the chance to play again, and Larry set up a kitty basket so the musicians could make a little money. Larry began to invite other musicians, but Punch was his favorite.

It may have seemed a comedown from those days in his youth when Punch was considered among the top trumpet players from New Orleans who made a name for himself in Chicago, but Punch never lost his pride, and you could always hear it in his horn. "Gypsy Lou" Webb, one of the many colorful characters in the French Quarter and co-publisher of *The Outsider*, wrote "Long Distance Blues" for him, which he recorded for Icon Records.

By the time I came to New Orleans, Larry's art gallery, leased to Allan and Sandra Jaffe, was named Preservation Hall. It was open seven nights a week with a kitty basket at the door; admission was one dollar. It could always be said that those who started it, by donating their time and talents at the gallery, were the musicians themselves. Punch's return to New Orleans prompted the start of his second career. During the 1960s he toured Japan with George Lewis, recorded for Atlantic Records, and made several short trips around the States.

On one of those Sunday afternoon "rehearsals," Punch was faced with three trumpet players from England, so he showed us how to play tunes like "Just a Closer Walk with Thee" in three-part harmony. "You play this," he'd say, then turn to the others and show them what to play. Finally he directed us all to play together. After we had learned several tunes in this manner, he told us to come down that night and sit in during the last set after midnight.

Where did he get his nickname? Although it seemed to describe the strong driving lead he played, his sister's name happened to be Judy. They were Punch and Judy, as in the famous and once popular puppet show.

There's a story about "Kid Punch," as he was known in the 1920s, and this is how trombonist Homer Eugene remembered it. Band contests used to be quite common, a good way to draw a crowd and sell tickets to a dance. The promoter of one of these events was not only Chinese but had an amusing stutter. When announcing Punch, he got stuck trying to get the name out: "Kid Punch-ee, Punch-ee, Punch-ee, Punch-ee, Punch-ee, Punch-ee Miller!" Homer was still chuckling at the memory of it fifty years later.

While his singing was identical to the recordings he made in the 1920s, Punch's dentures and the corn on his lip from years of blowing with a lot of lip pressure caused him to fluff notes quite

Punch Miller, Colin McCurdy, Clive Wilson, and B. Minter in 1964. Photo: Dan Lehrer, used by permission of Preservation Hall.

frequently. Yet toward the end of his life, Punch was able to spend a month in New York State with Albert "Doc" Vollmer who worked on his dentures to prevent them from slipping. At the same time Punch moved his embouchure over to the side of his corn and, once again, was able to play as he wanted. His final concert at the New Orleans Jazz & Heritage Festival in 1971, with Raymond Burke on clarinet, Emanuel "Manny" Sayles on banjo, Don Ewell on piano, and Freddie Kohlman on drums, brought the house to a standing ovation. He was terrific!

Punch and Clive in 1964 behind Preservation Hall. Photo: Dan Lehrer, used by permission of Preservation Hall.

A DREAM COME TRUE

I wasn't born in New Orleans, but I came as soon as I could.
—Overheard at a party in New Orleans

In some ways you could say New Orleans was an oasis from America. Or perhaps you could say it was a part of America that somehow had been forgotten and remained old-fashioned, a cultural backwater with its own ways and eccentricities. Exotic to me, it is situated on a piece of land claimed from the primeval swamp opposite a crescent-shaped curve in the Mississippi River, curving around an old suburb of New Orleans called Algiers. Under siege by the water that surrounds her, and in olden days, by the frequent yellow fever epidemics in the long hot summers, life for her inhabitants has always been a fragile and hence precious commodity, to be enjoyed as much as possible in the present, never sure how long it will last.

I'll never forget the carefree charm of the French Quarter, the site of the original settlement of 1718. A self-contained community, it had black and white families, children, teachers, artists and eccentrics, dockworkers and shopkeepers. It had its own school, fish market, brewery, meeting hall, and three convents—one only a block away from the longshoreman bars on the riverfront—a cinema, an undercover bookie joint with a secret, direct telephone line to every racetrack in the country, the St. Louis Cathedral at one end of Orleans Street and the Morning Star Baptist Church at the other.

Sadly, the French Quarter gradually changed. In the mid-Sixties, Bourbon Street's nightclub strip barely extended to St. Peter Street; the rest was residential, quiet and dark at night. St. Peter Street was fairly busy as it connected Bourbon Street to Jackson Square and the Mississippi. Pat O'Brien's was always there, with Preservation Hall right next door. The Café du Monde by the river stayed open all night. Most of the Quarter was old and unrenovated, a cheap place to live. Being residential, the stores catered to the families that lived there—a fishmonger, hardware and grocery stores, a fishing tackle store, everything you might need. But most of all what lingers in my mind is a kind of humid, dense blanket of air, saturated with the smells of the malt from Jax Brewery, roasting coffee, and the scents of flowering jasmine spilling over the brick-walled courtyards. No wonder I fell in love with the place.

And then there was the street music. Besides Sister Gertrude and her small gospel group, dressed in white uniforms, that played most days on the corner of Royal and St. Peter Streets, there was Babe Stovall playing his guitar and singing for tips. He was a former farm laborer from Mississippi, the genuine article.

All my subsequent nights were spent at Preservation Hall and Dixieland Hall, where I met many other fans and musicians as well as local French Quarter characters. One of those fans, a white-haired and bearded poet from Mississippi, also a civil rights activist, was John Beecher, a descendent from Harriet Beecher Stowe, who wrote *Uncle Tom's Cabin.* John happened to be a friend of the director of the Tulane University Medical Research Center and talked him into giving me a summer job, where I assisted an electronics engineer.

Trumpeter George Colar, better known as "Kid Sheik" from his youth in the 1920s when he wore "sheik" suits, took a special interest in visitors like me. Sheik had been on tour in England the year before and loved every minute of it. Not one of the better trumpet players in town, he was certainly the most friendly, and one of the first New Orleans musicians to tour as a guest with a British band.

Buster's Bar and Restaurant, Orleans and Burgundy Streets in the French Quarter. Photo: John Edser, used by permission.

He took me along to play on one of his gigs practically the first time we met, a social evening at an African American Masonic hall on Orleans Avenue just outside the French Quarter, across the street from Picou's Bar, once owned by the clarinetist Alphonse Picou. The line-up was quite unusual, with Noon Johnson on the "bazooka" (a homemade slide bass instrument played like a trombone), "Achie" Minor on banjo, and Sheik on trumpet.

"How d'you play second trumpet?" I asked (this was before those lessons with Punch).

"Just make anything that fits, heh, heh, heh!" laughed Sheik. His infectious good humor made me feel quite at home.

We met at Buster's, a bar and restaurant on the corner of Burgundy and Orleans streets. Where else would we have met? It was a crossroad where musicians frequently stopped by to get a drink before or after a gig. Buster Holmes welcomed one and all with his philosophy of feeding the hungry of the world. Serving very reasonably priced soul food, it suited my budget. A plate of red

Harold Dejan. Photo: Clive Wilson collection.

beans and rice was only twenty-six cents! Add a pork chop, or hot sausage, and it was seventy-five cents. Slow Drag Pavageau sat in a corner most afternoons, nursing a can of beer. He liked company, although old age had made his consonantless speech almost unintelligible. One evening, we were walking over to Preservation Hall when Drag suddenly announced: "I told Barbara Reid: you want to preserve this music? Call it Preservation Hall!"

But who is Barbara Reid? I silently asked myself.[1]

Kid Sheik also played regularly with the Eureka and Olympia brass bands, so he introduced me to Harold Dejan, the leader of the Olympia. After only a few weeks, Harold asked me to sit in with his band on the Young Men Olympians' parade and a month later, the Jolly Bunch parade.[2] He even drove down to the French

Quarter to pick me up. It was just after eight on a Sunday morning and the day was already heating up when the bell rang:

"I'm coming," I shouted down to him. "Give me a minute!"

"Take your time," he replied. "But hurry up and make it fast!"

Moments later, as I slid into his Ford Mustang, I added: "Thanks for the ride."

"That's alright," he smiled. "It's my nature."

That was Harold. I realized later—like Jelly Roll Morton on his recordings, who exclaimed such lines as "You're so dumb you must be the President of the Deaf and Dumb Society!"—this was typical New Orleans repartee.

We started at nine in the morning, following behind the "first line" of club members in their bright yellow shirts, gold sashes, and all carrying baskets of yellow flowers. It was a beautiful, colorful sight. In August, when the temperature and humidity soared into the mid-nineties, I quickly learned to conserve as much energy as possible. Kid Sheik coached me in that. As there were five trumpet players in all, we took turns playing choruses, perhaps two at a time, to pace ourselves. Time seemed to stand still as the sun rose to its zenith, beating down on us. Booker T's bass drumming provided a constant pulse throughout the day, a deep throb coming up through the street to my feet and to the "second line" dancers who thronged around us and all over the sidewalks. Although we had frequent stops for drinks and sandwiches at various neighborhood bars, the day seemed to stretch on forever. My clothes were soon wet through with sweat and my aching feet told me the day would never end. Yet that beat and the spirit of the dancers kept me moving. There was one dancer in particular who stands out in my memory. Of medium dark brown complexion with bright blue eyes, he was poetry in motion.

We wound up at five in the evening at the Caldonia in the Tremé section of town, where we managed to play a couple more numbers for the bar crowd. I had to put ice on my swollen lip to play a few more notes. How these older men carried it off amazed me, most

Clive sitting in with the Olympia Brass Band, 1964. Photo: Jules Cahn, gifted by Cahn to Clive Wilson. Used by permission.

of them in their sixties at the time—Booker T approaching eighty! I was totally exhausted, but so happy to be in the middle of it all. Kid Sheik turned to me and said: "You played the whole parade! You must be the first!" We finished our beers and limped home.

MEETING DICK ALLEN

Just a few days after arriving in New Orleans I made my first visit to the Archive of New Orleans Jazz[3] at Tulane University. A man who turned out to be Paul Crawford was bent over a typewriter, headphones on, transcribing interviews.

"I'm from England," I said, "and I've come to see Dick Allen."

"Well, you wouldn't want to be disappointed!" he replied. The implication that a nine-thousand-mile round trip would otherwise be wasted was not lost on me, but Paul's dry wit was unexpected and atypical. Paul escorted me to the cafeteria where we found Dick Allen at lunch.

After showing me around the little room into which the Archive was crammed in those days, Allen suggested we meet the following afternoon, a Saturday, for what he laughingly termed his "French Quarter Walking Tour"—a very personal initiation into a world he obviously loved. Dick Allen's tour took us past sights that had significance only for the avid New Orleans jazz fan. There was the barbershop on Burgundy Street, photographed by Ralston Crawford, which was displayed on the front cover of a Riverside LP. It was cater-corner across the street from Buster's Restaurant. Just up the street, sitting on his stoop, was the old retired cornet player Tom Albert, who began playing in bands around 1904. A contemporary of Bunk Johnson and Manuel Manetta, he had many stories to tell of Buddy Bolden, Manny Perez, and others from the very beginnings of jazz history.

Passing by the Morning Star Baptist Church in the 900 block of Burgundy Street, where Slow Drag's wife Annie Pavageau played the organ and directed the choir, we made our way over to the clarinetist Raymond Burke's shop near the corner of Bourbon and Dumaine. Little more than a hole in the wall, it was stuffed with every kind of collectible and bric-a-brac, including a few of his 30,000 78s. Raymond used the shop as a place to store his own junk more than anything else, for like all compulsive collectors, he hated to part with anything he had spent time looking for. He would rather trade than sell. The local fire chief once declared the shop a hazard and had him clean it out. Poor Raymond had to bring everything out of the store and stack it on the street. A modest crowd gathered to look over the treasures that had lain hidden for years, and Raymond sold so much that day that he almost had a nervous breakdown.

Passing through Pirate Alley, where William Faulkner lived and wrote *New Orleans Sketches* during 1925, we took a short break at the Napoleon House. Originally allocated for Bonaparte himself, it was a wonderful bar that had not changed much through the years. All the while Allen, being the Anglophile he was, delighted in showing off his knowledge of British humor by keeping up a running commentary peppered with lines from Spike Milligan, Tony Hancock, and Peter Sellers. *The Goon Show* was broadcast locally for several years, so Allen was quite at home with that type of craziness.

We finished the tour with a sandwich at the Bourbon House, the French Quarterites' nearest equivalent to a local pub. On what was then a quiet corner at Bourbon and St. Peter Streets, it was the place to meet everyone you wanted to see, from Gypsy Lou Webb, Bob Greenwood, Max Clevenger, Tennessee Williams—all the characters. It was everyone's front room, in a way. As Joanne Clevenger, married to Max, who was a member of the New Orleans Society for the Preservation of Traditional Jazz, recently reminded me: "We didn't have answer machines and email as we do today. We just went to the Bourbon House around four in the afternoon to make all our arrangements." The old French Quarter was like that.

Service by Robert was notoriously slow but the locals loved him for it. Tourists who accidentally wandered into his domain frequently became irate when he appeared to ignore them for fifteen, twenty, even thirty minutes. "Can't you see I'm busy?" Robert would say. To be in a hurry was a sure sign of coming from an alien world.

That night we went to eat at a neighborhood seafood restaurant on Elysian Fields called Wallace and Raoul's. We were surprised to find musicians Abbie and Merritt Brunies there and, while we were talking to them, in walked the trombonist Emile Christian. "I was in England in 1919 with the Original Dixieland Jazz Band," he told me upon being introduced. "I played for the King and Queen!" Emile Christian went on to say he left the ODJB while they were in Paris, staying over for the next ten years. Later I was to play with him in several pick-up bands. He was a well-schooled trombonist who nevertheless retained the same basic tailgate style he had acquired before 1920.

The advantage of knowing Dick Allen was that he kept in touch with everyone and everything that was going on. The next weekend, on a Sunday, he invited me to go with him to a party in the backyard of a part-time trumpet player named Leon Bageon. Leon assembled his band for the occasion and also invited his boss from his day job, which turned out to be quite embarrassing for us all. This man's behavior was patronizing and obnoxious. Besides us, he was the only white man there, and unlike everyone else, had no manners. Leon kept everything under control and simply got the man drunk on peach-flavored brandy. Thankfully, he left early.

The highlight of the day for me was listening to this music played simply for fun in an informal setting.[4] The music was warm and relaxed, yet punctuated by the ebullient drumming of Dave Bailey, who played in a pre-1920s style on a kit that was of the same vintage. He had a single-tension bass drum with a picture of a dancing couple under a palm tree painted on the front head, and a quartet of tuned cowbells. The Chinese cymbal was hanging by a leather thong from an old-fashioned horizontal cymbal arm, and Dave achieved a variety of effects by several methods of choking it. I can only describe his drumming as ecstatic and, indeed, Dave appeared to be in ecstasy as he played. With accents and varied percussive effects all over the drum kit, he played in a continuous, spontaneous fashion. Sounding experimental, his style derived from an early period in the development of jazz, yet contained elements thought to be modern, according to Dick Allen, in common with another legendary New Orleans drummer, Ed Blackwell. I have heard something similar played by Baby Dodds on Jelly Roll Morton's recordings of "Hyena Stomp" and "Billy Goat Stomp," which Dodds himself describes as ". . . in Spanish rhythm like so many of the numbers used to be played in New Orleans."[5]

I was going to work at Tulane University's Medical Research Center five days a week, which paid the minimum wage of $1.50/hour, a living wage then. The equivalent today would be $15.00/hour. I met interesting folks there, too. The electronics engineer, Mike, whom I was supposed to help, was a kind of genius, building monitoring equipment for all the doctors, such as equipment to measure the level of anesthesia during operations. So I saw quite a few things that I wasn't accustomed to. For example, they used dogs to experiment with heart machines so that one day they could do open heart surgery. And across Lake Pontchartrain in Covington, they had a large enclosure where they were experimenting on the behavior of monkeys with electrodes implanted in their brains. It made me feel quite sick. Someone mentioned the possibility of its application in mind control one day in the future. I went to the primate center with Mike once, but they wouldn't let me past reception as it was all very hush-hush research. Much later I heard that the man in charge of this research was known as Dr. Frankenstein by his colleagues and all the staff. One of the staff later told me he was experimenting also with implanted electrodes in the mentally ill.

One of the doctors we worked with, in a moment of regret, told me he thought the only area of real creativity left in society was in raising a family, in being a parent. I had a sense of what he meant. However, he wasn't a musician. Music and the arts qualify, too.

Happily, all the people I remember working with were very pro-integration. But in those first few weeks after the Civil Rights Act, things moved slowly and deliberately. There was a restaurant next door where we used to get our lunch, and the day came to integrate it. We all went together with our black secretary Pauline, to show solidarity. As she was quite beautiful, the Greek owner used to kid me about wanting to see her after work: "You want cloudy weather," he'd say, "cloudy weather!" He probably meant *he* wanted cloudy weather so he could take her out without being seen. That's the way it was.

I was lucky to get the job, and lucky enough to get off early on a couple of occasions when there was a recording session taking place in San Jacinto Hall in Tremé, just north of the French Quarter. It was the same place where Bill Russell had recorded Bunk Johnson in the 1940s. I took off after lunch and hurried over to the once proud hall, now in a very dilapidated state, to find a great band of, to me, musical giants.[6] Sitting in a line—stage right to left: drums, trombone, trumpet, trumpet, clarinet, banjo, and bass—on the old bandstand with a wooden railing around it, they sweated away in the heat, stripped down to their T-shirts. The producers had decided to use two trumpets instead of the regular one, played by "Kid Thomas" Valentine and Ernie Cagnoletti. Jim Robinson appeared to be the leader. Amplified by the acoustics of the hall, the band played with enormous power. To my mind it was too much echo for clarity, but the producers were recreating a bit of history when the hall, besides being the site of Bill Russell's recordings of Bunk Johnson, was used for dances on a regular basis.

Afterward, the bass player Slow Drag came over to me and shook his head. When I asked what was wrong, he said:

"You know what's wrong!"

"What do you mean?"

"*You* know what's wrong!" was all he'd say, shaking his head again. I wasn't sure what he meant because it sounded wonderful to me. Yet . . . perhaps he meant that the two trumpet players were not really compatible? Or perhaps that neither of the trumpet players knew who was to play the lead and who the second part? It might have been that he suspected the two different producers were each going to issue a separate LP for the price of one? Who knows? But whatever it was, I felt honored that Slow Drag had taken me into his confidence and assumed I had the musical sense to know what the others were missing or ignoring.

A TALE OF GEORGE GUESNON

Realizing that I was a complete beginner and not able to reproduce anything like the music I was hearing every night, I felt quite helpless. My early lessons with Owen Bryce were of no use. Although he had made me aware of chords and scales, I was not familiar enough with them and had no idea how to use them creatively when improvising. Nothing I had picked up from Bryce seemed to work. My attempts at variations came out in a mechanical way and sounded lame. What were the musicians doing to sound so strong, so authoritative?

"How long does it take?" I naively asked Bill Russell once.

"Oh, it takes time," he responded warmly, adding: "I know another trumpet player who couldn't play anything when he first came here in the Fifties, but he sounds pretty good now."

For three dollars an hour I took weekly lessons from George Guesnon (pronounced Gay-No), the self-proclaimed master of the tenor banjo. "Do just what I tell you and you'll be great!" he would say. "If all my 'scholars' did just that, they'd all be great; ain't that right?" His drummer Alex Bigard, who was sitting across the room, readily agreed. "Yeah, that's right, George."

Bigard and Guesnon, close friends and a rhythmic team, played regularly at Preservation Hall in what was undoubtedly the hottest band I remember. With John "Capt." Handy on alto sax, Joseph La Croix "DeDe" Pierce on cornet, Dolly Adams on piano, and Alex Bigard on drums, they just ripped into every number as if it was their last. After midnight they played nothing but the blues.

Guesnon concentrated on teaching me to play several of his single-string banjo solos on trumpet, memorizing them note for note. His favorite examples to use were "Should I Reveal" and "I'm Confessing That I Love You." In spite of the apparent limitations of his teaching method, Guesnon stressed, time and again, that his improvisations involved first playing the melody of each phrase followed by a "broken chord," that is, an arpeggio of the harmony in the gaps of the melody.

"Creole George" Guesnon, 1965. Photo: Clive Wilson collection.

For each phrase you returned to the melody, or at least a part of it, then broke up the harmony in the gap before the next phrase. After the lesson, Guesnon loved to play selections from his recordings. I remember noticing on one of these occasions that Kid Howard was, indeed, improvising in this manner. The melody, Guesnon added, had to be played with expression, with a deliberate use of vibrato, glissandi, and tonal color. Although this marked the beginning of a shift away from my initial concepts acquired from Owen Bryce, I felt quite lost, and with my limited technique, playing the music with any kind of conviction seemed impossible.

A few years later, not long before Guesnon died, I went to see him again accompanied by Dave Duquette, a banjo-playing friend from Connecticut. Although Guesnon was suffering quite badly from emphysema, his pride in his ability was undiminished.

"You see you can learn all the chords you want . . . ," he said, strumming as he spoke, ". . . and pick all the single string solos in the world . . . ," adding a few phrases typical of him, ". . . but you'll never have this!"

He laughed and simply began playing rhythm. The timing and springy feel of his beat arose from deep within him, a throbbing pulse that resonated from wall to wall of his old wood-framed house. I still remember him as we left, standing on his stoop flashing a big smile, his gold teeth glinting in the setting sun. He had made his point, and we were never to be quite the same again.

The memories of that summer—listening to music every night of the week and all day on the weekends—have never left me. Dixieland Hall featured the bands of Papa French and the legendary Paul Barbarin. Preservation Hall rotated their bands: "Sweet Emma the Bell Gal" Barrett with Percy and Willie Humphrey on the trumpet and clarinet, Punch Miller with Raymond Burke on the clarinet, Billie and DeDe Pierce, Jim Robinson, George Lewis, George Guesnon, and the amazing Kid Thomas. Besides a few private gigs that some musicians played, these venues provided the only place they worked in public. But for these venues opening in the early 1960s, their music might have died out.

One of the most extraordinary people I met was Papa John Joseph, who played the bass with Punch. He had toured Japan with George Lewis in 1963, where he celebrated his eighty-eighth birthday. He told me he began playing music when he was fourteen years old (in 1888!), had played with Buddy Bolden and King Oliver, and was the first to play saxophone in a New Orleans band in 1912. I heard later that on January 22, 1965, after finishing the gig at Preservation Hall with none other than "When the Saints Go Marching In," Papa John turned to the pianist Dolly Adams and said: "That piece just about did me in." He promptly collapsed across her lap and died.

REFLECTIONS

As my summer drew to a close at the end of September, I returned to New York to take the student charter flight back to the familiar world I had left behind in Britain. Riding the bus again for a couple of days, I had time to reflect on the whole experience of my visit in New Orleans. I realized I hadn't known what to expect. Recordings had not given me a picture of how the musicians feel about their music, of their attitude to life, of whom and what they are playing for, of how their music fits into the life of the city. I had to drop all my preconceived notions about playing New Orleans jazz.

Back in Britain, I had been learning to play the music of another culture and another era. When I listened to recordings, which are like snapshots frozen in time, I didn't get the inside picture directly; I could only guess at it, if I thought about it at all. In the translation of live music to vinyl, so much is lost, and the environment from which it springs is entirely hidden. What is going on in the minds of the performers? How do they feel? What contributes to their spirited sounds? Louis Armstrong once said that whenever he plays his horn, "I just close my eyes and think of those good old times back in New Orleans." He was feeling and visualizing, perhaps, the whole experience of his youth—the joys, pain, hard work, goofing off, singing for tips on the streets, eating gumbo and red beans and rice, and listening to the older players. It's all there, implicit in every note he played. Kid Sheik, commenting about legendary trumpet players he loved to hear when he was young, used to say: "Wooden Joe played *direct*! Chris Kelly played *direct*! Heh! heh! heh!" He laughed. He meant they played their feelings spontaneously, directly from the heart, with a strong emotional conviction.

In trying to reproduce the music I loved, as we did back in Britain, I could not play from the experiences of those whose music I was copying. Inevitably there was something missing. Speaking for myself: it wasn't *my* music, I wasn't genuinely using it to express myself at this stage; I was pretending to express what I thought I heard in the recorded music. I was playing secondhand, whereas the New Orleans originals were playing firsthand. So I discovered a paradox: that to play authentic jazz, I had to play myself, my own ideas, yet I needed to listen to the New Orleans musicians to find out how to do that in their style. This involved imitation, and in that I was made welcome. As there were few young, indigenous musicians in the 1960s who were interested in the traditional jazz of their elders, I was made doubly welcome simply because I *was* interested. The few locals who were interested included trombonists Fred Lonzo, Scotty Hill, and Lester Caliste, sousaphone and bassist Walter Payton, twelve-year-old drummer Shannon Powell, and teenage clarinetist Tommy Sancton, the only local white youngster eager to learn the music he heard at Preservation Hall.

However, I think the principal reason that jazz pilgrims like myself were so encouraged by the older African American musicians is that they knew and sensed that we hadn't grown up in a segregated society, with all the baggage that entailed. We looked up to them, and they responded with considerable relief that here was a white person they didn't need to be defensive with—in fact, they were my heroes. They could talk to us as equals, without any fear. They could relax in our company. This being the first time in their lives that it was legal to socialize with a white person in their own town, they made us feel at home.

Although I suspect that some of the time they felt flattered by my attempt at imitation, I later learned that New Orleans musicians have at least one golden rule: don't copy, find your own style. "Don't steal my stuff!" is a deep-seated feeling. In New Orleans, you do not get respect for sounding like someone else, no matter how good you are. So you must be patient and give it time. But the point I want to make is that in Britain, you get praised if you can imitate Kid Howard, George Lewis, or Kid Thomas. In New Orleans, you do not. I once asked Kid Howard if he could show me how various trumpet players played who had influenced *him* in his early years back in the 1920s. He refused.

"I used to play like Chris Kelly, Buddy Petit, Guy Kelly, Sam Morgan, Louis Armstrong, all of them," he said angrily. "But now I just play myself."

Many years later, I received good advice from the clarinetist Herb Hall: "Don't listen to any one musician all the time," he said, "especially when you are a beginner. Listen to all the guys if you want to sound like yourself."

And if you follow that advice, it does come together in a new way eventually. In any case, when I learn something from another musician, it still comes out with my tone, my rhythm, and hopefully becomes integrated into a broad spectrum of influences.

Back in Britain, I was aware of several different attitudes among those who played traditional jazz. One was: "We'll never play *real* New Orleans jazz; we weren't born there," which is negative, self-defeating, and even depressing for some. The other was: "I don't care about that; I just play whatever I want." My attitude was: "I'll give it a go and see what happens."

Jazz was different in New Orleans. I don't mean to imply that it's no good anywhere else, just that traditional jazz or Dixieland was played differently in other places. The very fact that New Orleans jazz wasn't concert music allowed the musicians to play with a different feel than, say, in Chicago or New York. Playing New Orleans jazz in New Orleans is a trade. Being hired as tradesmen to play background music as part of another function allowed the musicians to stay unpretentious, relaxed, and yet open to spontaneity. That appealed to me. When I first arrived I used to think they played everything at a slower pace because of the heat. It *was* mid-summer, after all. And although I'm sure that's partly true, the musicians I met in New Orleans were craftsmen, expressing themselves best in the easy rolling two-beat groove that suited the music. They played with an unhurried feel, of a time far removed from the current pace of life. Yet by generating a powerful pulse, they could build excitement. Their music had an inner strength, was danceable yet ratty at the same time.

I realize now that these musicians did not think the way I did when I was a beginner. In contrast to playing music as heard on recordings, they played songs that people wanted to hear in the way they liked to play them—the way they had learned to play from their elders. In those days with a revival of interest in their kind of jazz—the sixties, seventies and eighties—they played songs for the most part that people *used* to want to hear when they were younger; popular tunes from the 1920s and 1930s, spirituals, and certain marches associated with the music. But their repertoire was never restricted to that. If they could make it fit into their style, they played whatever new popular song came along. In his youth, Bunk Johnson was so famous for playing what people wanted to hear that he was called "Willie the Pleaser."

When I started out in Britain we played the songs *we* wanted, whereas in New Orleans everyone played "Hello Dolly," "Cabaret," "What a Wonderful World," whatever was popular. The first time I went to see Manuel Manetta in his home in Algiers in 1966, I could hardly believe my ears when he played the latest hit tune from a Broadway musical on his beat-up old piano. "Have you heard this?" he announced. "'Seventy-six Trombones.' It's a great song!"

That's hardly a tune I associate with jazz, and perhaps that's the point. New Orleans jazz was originally dance music, a new way of playing the tunes of the day. So the idea was to play the songs that were popular, but play them "hot," with syncopation, with a lilting swing, and with variation. The so-called jazz repertoire emerged gradually over time. In New Orleans, music was everywhere and at every event, which is still true today. An integral part of the social fabric, it is played for functions: a wedding, a parade, a dinner party, or a dance. And so it was never on the concert stage or played fast. And when people dance to the music they become part of the whole experience. There is no pressure on the musicians, and their music is relaxed, informal, and joyous. They perform for others to enjoy themselves. As the trombonist Jim Robinson would say: "I play to make people feel happy, and that makes me happy."

In a way, it's like the music at a Sanctified church, where the distinction between the musicians and the congregation is blurred. Everyone joins in; everyone is part of the event. I experienced that myself at the St. Philip Church of God in Christ, which was just outside the French Quarter in Tremé—but not during my first visit, a couple of years later. I went to hear Sidney Brown, who had recorded on string bass with the Sam Morgan band back in the 1920s. He was known also as "Jim Little" because he was Jim Robinson's nephew. Having "got religion" after experiencing a healing, he would play only in church. But his style was unchanged from forty years earlier.

I went everywhere—listening to it all.

And so my summer had turned out to be quite a revelation. But the adventure wasn't over yet. On my return via New York, I stayed a few days in Brooklyn with Trev and Judith Leger, friends of Dick Allen whom I had met in New Orleans. On my second night in town I was able to hear the great Louis Armstrong for the first time in person, a special appearance at the Metropole for two nights only. How would he sound in person, I wondered? Listening up close to a variety of trumpet players in New Orleans had given me a fine appreciation for their varied tone colors, of how each player's tone was an intimate expression of his identity. Now I would hear Louis's. I stood at the bar about fifteen feet in front of his horn, listening to him directly without amplification. What a sound! It was everything I had come to expect from a New

Orleans man, and yet extraordinary. No recording quite captures the breadth, brilliance, and intensity that came across live. That's where I first met the photographer Jack Bradley, who happened to be standing next to me at the bar. He bought me a beer and yelled and clapped through every set. Later, I found out he was a personal friend and "Armstrong's greatest fan."

A TALE OF SISSLE AND BLAKE

By chance, my stop in New York coincided with a once-in-a-lifetime opportunity to see a most unusual show at Fordham University. Dick Allen, who also happened to be visiting New York, and the guitarist Danny Barker, joined us for the evening. It was my first meeting with Danny and I remember him talking of his plan to move back to New Orleans within the year.

Produced by none other than Noble Sissle and Eubie Blake, the performance was a re-creation of a minstrel show. It played only twice, in 1964, at Fordham University and the YMCA in Harlem. All the entertainers were in their sixties, seventies, and eighties, and all were veterans of the stage. The only difference between this minstrel show and the original, according to Sissle, was that the performers were not in blackface. As I remember, Noble Sissle rambled on a bit too long in the prologue about the cultural importance of the minstrel show in the African American experience, but he emphasized that it provided almost the only opportunity for black entertainers to enter the stage, and most importantly, that all minstrelsy was satire.

There was nothing slow about the show itself, however. With an energy that belied their age, the "Gentlemen of the Circle," as they were termed, sang songs, told jokes, and danced their way through the first act, frequently ending up a number doing the splits, just like thirty, forty, or fifty years before. Their style of humor, so similar to Cajun jokes, poked plenty of fun at themselves and also reminded me of the "shaggy-dog" stories I grew up with. Did this style of joke, as well as the "straight man/funny man" routine, originate with the minstrel show? In spite of Sissle's emphasis on culture, everyone clearly was exhilarated and overjoyed to relive these moments in front of an audience.

We met the band during the intermission. A high-pitched voice behind me greeted Dick Allen: "Hi Dick, how's New Orleans?"

Turning, I saw a man who looked like a garden gnome, only a little bigger. It was the same speaking voice that sang "Gee Baby, Ain't I Good to You" on the McKinney Cotton Pickers recording, belonging, of course, to Don Redman. A giant in the history of American jazz, Redman is widely considered to be one of the seminal figures in the evolution of big band arranging. His band played an entirely support-ive role in the production except, unlike a pit orchestra, they were quite visible on a platform to the side of the stage.[1]

The second half of the program began with a short feature from the band, the only time they played without written arrangements. It was sophisticated, swinging jazz, but I remember being mildly dis-appointed at the time since no one took a really hot solo. However, their discipline was perfectly suited to the occasion. At some point in the show Luckey Roberts played a couple of stride solos in spite of suffering badly from arthritis in his hands. Frisco Bowman came on and executed a most incredible drum solo using only the snare drum. Another member of the "Circle" brought the house down with a poignant rendition of "The Best Things in Life Are Free" on the musical saw! I think Dick Allen thought this the funniest moment of the evening. And Strawberry Russell told a long, drawn-out shag-gy-dog story that had everyone doubled up with laughter.

Near the end of the evening, Sissle and Blake performed a medley of their biggest hits including "I'm Just Wild about Harry," and Eubie Blake played a few of his piano compositions like "Charleston Rag." Full of fun and exuberance in typical Sissle and Blake fashion, this was, I suspect, the final theatrical production of their amazing part-nership. Five more years would pass before John Hammond recorded a double album—*The Eighty-Six Years of Eubie Blake* (Columbia C2S 847)—with Noble Sissle on vocals. The subsequent attention accorded Eubie propelled him into his second career. "If I'd known I was going to live this long, I'd have taken better care of myself!" he was to tell Johnny Carson on *The Tonight Show*.[2]

Before leaving for Britain, I heard Red Allen again. He was burning up every song with his usual red-hot routine at the Metropole, playing standards and show tunes. I went up to him on his break: "Mr. Allen," I began. "I've just spent the summer in New Orleans and played the Jolly Bunch Parade with the Olympia Brass Band!" He looked a little taken aback, then his eyes lit up and he gave me a big broad smile.

"Oh! So you had a *good* time!"

Red didn't have much more to say, but he showed me how he felt. When he returned to the stage behind the long bar, he announced: "Now I'm going to play something from my hometown New Orleans: 'Just a Closer Walk with Thee.'"

BACK IN BRITAIN

Strange as it may seem, not once during the three-year physics course was I given any indication of what a physicist could do with a degree after graduation. As I did not see myself as a research physicist, nor yet a jazz musician, I returned to Newcastle University for a one-year teacher training course that was thankfully considerably easier than physics. With more time simply to enjoy life, I was able to divide my activity between my studies and trumpet playing. Belonging now to a select group of jazz fans that had actually lived for a time in New Orleans, I knew I would go back some day, but when?—an open question. There was an undeniable, new dimension in my life and in my trumpet playing, amateurish though it was. Now I, too, could close my eyes and imagine I was back there again, sitting in with Dejan's Olympia Brass Band, blowing in the hot, humid summer.

October was already getting chilly with a persistent cold wind off the North Sea, but Newcastle is a friendly enough place. I remember sitting in with a local jazz band led by trumpeter Clem Avery, who was always encouraging, and eventually playing my own regular spot on Tuesday nights at a pub called the Cornerhouse. On occasion, I'd hitchhike to London for a long weekend to play with Mike Casimir's Paragon Brass Band. Very much an accepted mode of travel in those days especially for students, hitchhiking was easy if you dressed fairly well and above all, wore your university scarf. I could predict how long it would take for the 280 miles to London (before motorways)—about eight hours.

One of those trips to London coincided with a visit by Harold Dejan, who was over for a tour with Barry Martyn's band. When Dejan asked Dan Pawson and myself to make a brass band recording with him, I felt like an old friend. Later in the year, George Lewis also toured with Martyn, and I heard him in Newcastle at a local club. He was playing magnificently and remembered me from the summer in New Orleans. And so I stayed connected to, yet distanced from, my New Orleans experience. Somewhere, several thousand miles away, I had another life, and other friends.

But the teaching practice in a classroom was a real struggle—actually, chaotic—and I soon realized it was not for me. So what was I to do instead? Computers and systems analysis interested me, so I applied for a job in that field, saying to myself that if I failed to get the job, I would return to New Orleans in the fall and work there. As the job did not materialize, my course was set for New Orleans once again. I planned on staying two years this time. My parents helped me out by giving me a summer job clearing the land around their new home in Shropshire, and by September I had enough money to buy a one-way Icelandic Air ticket to New York, which was half the price of the airlines that flew direct.

"Are you sure you want to go back to New Orleans just now?" my father asked. "They've been hit by a hurricane." It was Hurricane Betsy.

But I was sure.

A RESIDENT ENGLISHMAN

"Ever since I can remember, it seems there has always been a resident Englishman in New Orleans," declared Larry Borenstein, his eyes gleaming behind his thick glasses. "Now it's your turn."[1]

Meeting so many friends from the year before at Preservation Hall each evening, I felt instantly at home on my return. Even Larry Borenstein, who held the lease on Preservation Hall and was notoriously tight with his money, bought me a cup of coffee. In addition, I met Bill Russell for the first time. It was he who had recorded and promoted the legendary Bunk Johnson in the 1940s.

It was apparent that I was one among many fans of the music to visit the city and that, for us, New Orleans is a kind of Mecca. With each succeeding year, more and more of us made the pilgrimage until it became a veritable deluge, with fans visiting from Sweden, Belgium, Norway, Britain, Japan, Germany, Italy, Canada, Australia, and other parts of the United States.

I met one of those "jazz pilgrims" on my first night back, a young piano player from Sweden named Lars Edegran. Within a few weeks we were sharing an apartment at 931 Royal Street in the heart of the French Quarter. There was no better place to live; it was cheap, convenient, and besides, Dick Allen, the curator of the Jazz Archive at Tulane University, lived across the street.

The debris from Hurricane Betsy was all cleaned up in the French Quarter, except for a few houses, hit by a twister, that were completely demolished. Yet the house next door might be untouched. The flooding in the Lower Ninth Ward below the Industrial Canal had receded—I was told there were three breaches in the levee (some things never change). But many of the residential areas, especially in the suburbs, were still full of piles of fallen tree limbs and garbage. As Lars and I needed some money fast, we enlisted in the cleanup crews. We worked ten-hour days at minimum wage, but it was so cheap to live that we only needed to work two days a week.

"You've integrated the cleanup crews for the first time!" chuckled Allan Jaffe, the manager of Preservation Hall.

About a month later I got an office job in the business district, working for an oil exploration company that paid double what I could have started out with in Britain. The job was not what I really wanted, but it suited me for six months or so. I saved most of my income and took a long vacation/adventure that lasted all the next summer. But I am jumping ahead of myself.

On my return in 1965, I immediately noticed that the number of tourists had increased dramatically, no doubt because of the end of segregation. The bands at Preservation Hall had grown to six and seven pieces, enabling Kid Thomas's band to be hired regularly one night a week. Punch Miller's band was moved to Sunday night, Slow Drag replacing the late Papa John Joseph on the bass. Under the strong, commanding lead of Punch, they used more harmony and head arrangements than usual. The band included George Lewis's drummer Joe Watkins, who played the way of his choice in two-beat (2/2 or "cut" time)—Lewis always demanded four-beat from his drummers—along with Raymond Burke on clarinet, Paul Crawford on trombone, Dolly Adams on piano, and Papa John Joseph on string bass. A year later, Johnny Wiggs was added on cornet.

By spending almost every night of the week at Preservation and Dixieland Halls, I became well known to the musicians. I joined the musicians' union when NBC-TV came to town that November to film a documentary. They wanted a scene with Lars, Tommy

Lars and Clive at 931 Royal Street, 1965. Photo: Clive Wilson collection.

Sancton, and me sitting in at Preservation Hall. We were news-
worthy, I guess, so Allan Jaffe, who ran the Hall, made the arrangements. "The gig pays," he said, "but you have to join the union."
So we joined Local 496, the black union local, to which Jaffe also
belonged. As we were mainly hanging out with African American
musicians, it was the natural local to join, and playing this job paid
for the initiation fees. Local 496 could then claim they had integrated, long before the merger with the white union. "Now you can
play with a better class of musicianers," said Kid Sheik.

And I *was* invited to sit in occasionally, but *working* as a musician in New Orleans was the furthest thing from my mind. I was
there to listen and learn.

Once a week for about five months I took lessons from the cornetist DeDe Pierce, who was delighted and happy to give them for
a very reasonable price. He and his wife Billie lived in the Seventh
Ward, in a small two-room house set behind a larger house on
the street. The room was quite dark and the walls badly needed

Part of the Louis James Footwarmers at New Orleans Union Station with dancer, 1966. Lawrence Trotter, Lars Edegran, Clive Wilson, Andrew Morgan. Photo: Clive Wilson collection.

painting, but DeDe had gone blind some years before and no longer noticed his surroundings. He sat on the double bed that took up most of the space and pulled out his old, rather worn silver cornet. Alternating lead and harmony, we played duets together on tunes like "Indian Love Call," "Love Song of the Nile," "and "Hindustan." After a while Billie would come in from the other room and accompany us on the piano that was against the wall by the kitchen—my own private concert.

I think my visits gave them something to do during the evening since their only gigs were at Preservation Hall. In fact, many of the older musicians were unable to get much work, and I wanted to hear as many of them as possible. Although I heard some at the neighborhood parades and some at private parties, often the only way was to visit a musician in his home. For that reason, Lars and I spent one afternoon playing music at the home of the bass player Louis James. "Old Man James," as he was known, surprised us both by asking us if we would form a band with him. Would we? We jumped at the chance! After many phone calls, we had our first rehearsal at the home of Lawrence Trotter, our drummer. Earl Humphrey came on trombone and Andrew Morgan on clarinet and tenor sax. These rehearsals, about two a month, were really small parties, with food and drink. Sometimes we held them at Morgan's house, sometimes at our guitarist Ernest Roubleau's, or James's house. We became quite a family, and even played occasionally for church fairs and dances. Earl's imagination got the better of him when he said I reminded him of his favorite trumpet player Lee Collins. I wish! At that time I was doing my best to play in the New Orleans style by memorizing everything I played.

A couple of years later, and not being sure how much longer I would live in New Orleans, I decided to record the band with the help of the staff at the Tulane Jazz Archive. At first, however, no one was interested in issuing the session since Andrew Morgan played the tenor sax and not the clarinet on most tracks. In the minds of several friends of mine who owned their own independent record labels, this session was not something they were looking for—they didn't like the sax. Ironically, the recording eventually found quite an appreciative audience, appearing successively on La Croix, Center, Biograph, and now 504 Records.

One day in December 1965, Andrew Morgan announced he was going to take over the Young Tuxedo Brass Band as the previous leader, Wilbert Tillman, had retired due to ill health. The next month I received a phone call on a Friday morning before I went to work. It was Morgan:

"Can you play a couple of funerals with me tomorrow and Sunday?" he asked.

"Well, yes, of course!" I replied. "But you know I've never even *seen* a funeral, let alone played in one."

He laughed. "That's OK; you know enough hymns to get by. The first one's uptown by Carrollton," he added. "I'll pick you up at ten. It's a black suit, white shirt, black tie, and a parade hat with black top. You got all that?"

Morgan was like a big, black Santa Claus, very jolly, and hugely optimistic, much more optimistic about my ability to play a funeral than I was. When I got there I found out he expected me to play the lead, as did both Kid Thomas and Reginald Koeller, the other trumpet players.

"Why me?" I asked.

"Well, you're Morgan's trumpet player," said Koeller.

"Kicks, man!" said Thomas.

And that's how I came to play lead trumpet on my first jazz funeral. Subsequently, Morgan brought in Thomas Jefferson to play lead trumpet and I moved over to second.

Little did I know it at the time, but those of us who were learning to play music in New Orleans witnessed the last years of an aspect of life in the city that has all but disappeared—the employment of traditional-style brass bands for a seemingly endless variety of occasions and events in the community, and the Young Tuxedo played its share of them. There were anniversary parades for "social aid and pleasure" clubs, funerals for Masonic lodges and burial societies, cornerstone layings and Sunday school parades for Baptist churches, all of which took place in the poorer, mostly African American sections of the city and across the river in Algiers and Gretna. Unlike the parades you see today, the second line was usually small. On the Sunday school parades the children, dressed in white, lined up in two rows behind the band in ascending order by height, followed by the lady church members, also in white, and finally the men in black suits. It was a beautiful sight. The parades were short by New Orleans standards, lasting less than two hours, but we often played for a party in the church hall afterwards where cake and Hawaiian punch would be served. Looking back, I remember that most weekends, when not rehearsing with Louis James, either I would go to see a parade or play in one. On one of those occasions, waiting for a parade to begin, I heard some black kids beating rhythms on a mail box by the side of the road.

"Listen to that," I exclaimed. "Sounds like Africa!"

The Young Tuxedo Brass Band, 1967. Albert "Loochie" Jackson, tb; Jerry Green, tuba; Earl Humphrey, tb; leader Andrew Morgan, ts; Ernest Poree, as; Thomas Jefferson, Reginald Koeller, Clive Wilson, tps; Lawrence Trotter, sd; Emile Knox, bd. Photo: Clive Wilson collection.

"Yes, it does," said one of the older New Orleans guys with me. "But I don't expect we'll be able to hear that much longer. It'll disappear now we have integration."

"Really? I don't believe it!" As it turned out, my friend was proved quite wrong, and today those African rhythms are more popular than ever, not only with the Mardi Gras Indians (as ever), but turning up in the funk bands and all the new brass bands in town.

Playing these parades with the Young Tuxedo Brass Band actually led to a change of heart about my life in New Orleans among members of my extended family back in Britain. Initially, many of them deplored the way they imagined my life to be in New Orleans. I had run away. Shouldn't I be working as a physicist in Britain? After all, the government had subsidized my university education. An uncle even spoke quite harshly to my mother once: how could she let me go off to another country and not take up a worthwhile job, as he saw it, in Britain? Wasn't I throwing my life away? My mother later told me she knew I had to make my own way in the world, even though she felt I had abandoned everyone.

But the *Daily Telegraph* saw a story in this. They had seen a TV special about music in America, and the New Orleans section included a funeral parade with the Young Tuxedo. Who was that Brit playing trumpet with the band? So they asked me to write something for them about my life. That piqued their interest further and they sent a reporter over to write the story and hired a photographer. When it came out in the *Daily Telegraph* Weekend Supplement early in 1968, all objections from family members evaporated. I went from being a renegade to a hero overnight. They were proud of me now. My mother said she felt vindicated.

Sometime in March 1966 my day job asked me to relocate to Houston, which was simply out of the question. So I lost that job. But right away I had a completely different offer via Sammy Rimington to join Bill Bissonette's Easy Riders Jazz Band in Connecticut. By this time Sammy had quit Ken Colyer's band in Britain, immigrating to the States. Jumping at the chance to work with Sammy, I said I'd give it a try for a month and see how it went. Being out of work, I was free to go.

But I decided to visit Chicago on the way, and hitched a ride with some members of the Salty Dogs, a band from Indiana, who dropped me off at a fork in the road about a hundred miles south of Chicago. It was just like that famous scene in the movie *North by Northwest*—flat farmland, not a house, not a tree, not anyone to be seen. Luckily, I was not buzzed by a crop duster, and a truck driver picked me up for the remainder of the journey.

I stayed a few nights on a couch at the home of record producer Bob Koester, who kindly showed me around several of the clubs in town. That's where I heard several bluesmen like Otis Rush, but also the New Orleans drummer extraordinaire Freddie Kohlman for the first time at a club called Jazz Limited. What a rhythm section it was! Emanuel Sayles, whom I knew from the year before

Kid Howard, 1962. Photo: Mike Casimir,
used by permission.

A TALE OF KID HOWARD[2]

Among the numerous wonderful musicians who I was privileged to listen to, there was yet one trumpet player whose playing and personality on stage was electrifying, whose passion and ability embodied the very essence of New Orleans trumpet, and that was Avery "Kid" Howard. His fiery playing had won him respect not only locally, but also in the surrounding parishes (counties are called parishes in Louisiana), across the United States, and overseas. His emotions were always close to the surface, and you felt the nervous tension in his playing, an excitement that seemed impatient to spill out of his horn. Emanating a sense of rhythm even when standing still, Howard played and sang with the fervor and excitement of a preacher at a revival meeting. I have seen him standing on a table, leading the crowd by clapping his hands, singing twenty or more verses to "Li'l

Liza Jane." There was a thrill in his playing, sometimes of anguish, sometimes of pure joy.

When I approached Kid Howard for trumpet lessons in late 1965, he declined but invited me to dinner instead. The house where he and Myrtis lived was on the corner of Ursulines and Burgundy Streets, a mere four blocks from my apartment. His cooking turned out to be as hot as his music, for he served up a very spicy roast chicken, marinated with hot chili peppers and basted to perfection.

Whether in praise of the musicians he played with or to let you know of something he didn't like, he was never afraid to speak his mind. Yet he was kind and encouraging to young musicians like myself who came to listen to him, and on several occasions invited me to sit in with Paul Barbarin's band, with whom he played at Dixieland Hall. I would play one number, then deliberately request "Over in the Gloryland." This brought Howard, who could never resist singing that spiritual, immediately back to the bandstand, and we would play first and second trumpets for the remainder of the set.

Unfortunately, the Kid had a drinking problem and, like several musicians I came to know over the years, passed away of cirrhosis of the liver in the spring of 1966.

The news rippled through the city, and such a large attendance was expected at his wake that it was scheduled for two nights. Most of his friends, relatives, Masonic lodge members, and admirers went to the funeral home on both nights, so it was packed. As drinks and sandwiches were served, the wake turned into a great social gathering at which many old friends became reacquainted, and newcomers to New Orleans like myself had the opportunity to meet countless musicians for the first time. Since then I have only attended one other wake (Uncle Lionel Batiste's) that lasted two days, and have never seen a funeral with such a large crowd. The banjoist George Guesnon remarked that Howard's funeral was the largest he had seen since Papa Celestin's in 1954.

Two brass bands, the Onward and the Olympia, were hired to play the funeral, and many other musicians were invited to join in, including myself with the Olympia. Danny Barker, sporting a huge unlit cigar in his mouth, was the grand marshal of the Onward.

We began by playing hymns in a subdued manner, playing softer and softer as we approached the Zion Hill Baptist Church. By now the crowd, both black and white almost equally mixed, was so dense that it was very difficult to get through. The closest any car could approach was four blocks from the church, which was filled to capacity. The service began and we waited outside.

With three preachers officiating, the service was long. When it was over, floral tributes began to be carried out, and the Olympia Brass Band struck up with "What a Friend We Have in Jesus." People were streaming out of the church, but still there was no sign of the casket. We stopped playing for a long time. Eventually we received a signal as the casket came into view, and we began playing "Just a Closer Walk with Thee." The Onward was gathered a block up the street, and the whole procession moved off as the bands played funeral dirges. The crowd pressed in and around us, making it difficult to play. After a few blocks, we parted into two and let the hearse and limousines pass through, which sped away to the Mount Olivet Cemetery where the Masons performed their last rites.

By this time the crowd in the second line was getting impatient for the parade back to the Caldonia, and a roar went up from the crowd as Milton Batiste sounded the signal on his trumpet. We kicked off with "When the Saints Go Marching In." With the Onward several blocks ahead of us, there was a sea of people, perhaps numbering five thousand, in front, behind, and all around us. Many danced with umbrellas, some black, some decorated, so many umbrellas going up and down in time with the music. I will never forget that sight, and I will never forget the thrill on hearing the sound of so many yelling out together in the breaks of "Whoopin' Blues."

It was late in the afternoon when we broke up at the Caldonia. George Finola came over to me carrying the gold-plated trumpet that Howard used in the last years of his life. It had belonged to Finola's uncle, and Howard liked it so much that Finola had lent it to him indefinitely. I loved the warm, thick, expressive sound that Howard had produced with this horn. George handed it to me, as he knew I tried to emulate the Kid.

"Play something," he said. I held it for a few moments, then tried a few phrases of "Over in the Gloryland," and handed it back to him. But in that moment I resolved to try to always keep something of Kid Howard's music alive in my own playing.

This was a day when each segment of society that was represented contributed to the event—the gospel singing in the church, the wailing of the bereaved family members, the somber funeral dirges, the incredible emotional release in the second line dancing after the hearse and mourners went off to the cemetery, and finally, the secret graveside rites of the Masons. It is the way New Orleans says goodbye to a much-loved and great musician. A spectator could very well wonder if the funeral, as in West African tradition, was the most important day in a man's life. Kid Sheik told me: "We cry at the birth, and rejoice at the death."

when he was working with Sweet Emma's band at Preservation Hall, played banjo and guitar, and the great Quinn Wilson, who had recorded with Jelly Roll Morton and Tiny Parham years before, played string bass and sousaphone.

I hitched out of Chicago as snow was beginning to fall.[3] It was a cold start, but before an hour was up I was on my way in the warm cab of another truck. This time I made it past Cleveland and just into Pennsylvania before getting stuck at an all-night rest stop around three in the morning. So I jumped on the Greyhound bus for New York when it came by.

Quite unexpectedly, the day came when I was able to put those "lessons" with DeDe Pierce to practical use. My stint with the Easy Riders happily coincided with a ten-day tour the band had booked with Billie and DeDe. I would sit out while DeDe played his first set, then join the band on second trumpet later in the evening. On several of DeDe's favorites, we both stood up and played his solo in two-part harmony, a real surprise to the audience! One of my fondest memories of that time was a party at the home of Fred and Filly Paquette—great jazz fans—where Billie entertained us on piano, singing the blues and several ribald songs besides. That was the night when their teenage son David decided to be a piano player himself.

A week later, after picking up a much better trumpet from a repair shop in Bridgeport, we played a short tour with the great Capt. John Handy on the alto sax. That tour included a recording session, which was eventually released from a rough mix on Jazz Crusade, then later on GHB BCD-325 as *Very Handy: Capt. John Handy and the Easy Riders Jazz Band*. We talked a lot about the late Kid Howard, and Handy showed me some of the riffs he used to play. Howard and Handy had a close musical affinity.

But after a month in Connecticut, I was bitten with the wanderlust. After all, I was completely free to do whatever I wanted, so I took a summer trip that included time in the Bahamas; in Jamaica, where I stayed with John Graham, an old school friend; and in Miami harbor, where I worked as a deckhand on a two-masted schooner alongside Keith, another Englishman I had met in New Orleans. Keith had a dream to buy a yacht and diving equipment to go in search of Spanish gold in the Caribbean. Although his plans fell through, he had obtained maps of the shipwrecks from the New Orleans Public Library. Eventually we found ourselves working on a fast motor yacht that the owner had used to ferry Cubans from Castro's Cuba to Florida. He claimed to be waiting for instructions from his New York associates to pick up "contraband coffee" from Venezuela—perhaps, but who knows? Though it entailed some danger, the two of us hung around for a while, thinking this would be exciting. But the trip never came through, and eventually I yearned to be back in New Orleans, listening to the wonderful music and playing my horn. I returned in September, and it wasn't long before I landed a day job in a bank as a computer programmer, working with Basic Assembly Language (BAL).

And I went right back to my original apartment at 931 Royal Street which I was sharing with Lars Edegran.

UNLIKELY CONNECTIONS: WILHELM REICH AND JFK

While working on the boat in Miami harbor, Keith and I met a couple of English girls who were traveling around the States. They had recently been through New Orleans and told me of Mike Brothers, who was building an orgone box to Wilhelm Reich's specifications, and a photographer called Matt Herron, also a fan of Reich, whose family they had stayed with. Being fascinated by Reich ever since coming across his writings while at university, I resolved to visit them both on my return. Mike Brothers and his wife Pat lived on Royal Street in the French Quarter and became my good friends. Mike proved to be quite an eccentric. Besides a Reich-designed orgone box and rain machine, he built amazing sculptures out of scrap metal. I'm not sure Louisiana was a good place to test the rain machine, however, as by late spring we tended to have afternoon thundershowers every day. But the orgone box was another story. After fifteen minutes sitting in it, I felt completely refreshed and rejuvenated.

At that time, many of us were questioning the Warren Commission's version of the Kennedy assassination, and I remember Matt Herron telling me he was doing some photographic work for a group that was investigating it, but he was not at liberty to say who they were. Another acquaintance of mine, Tom Bethell, jazz fan and onetime schoolteacher, showed a keen interest in working with this group, so I introduced him to Matt who put him in touch with Jim Garrison, the New Orleans District Attorney. Fairly soon after that, the investigation was leaked to the press, and Garrison was forced to go public.

MY NEW FAMILY

There was a network in those years. The musicians knew each other, the fans knew each other, and the fans knew the musicians. It was a big family!
—Dick Allen, curator of the Hogan Jazz Archive in New Orleans

As international travel became more common, and New Orleans an easier place to visit, an ever-increasing tide of jazz fans from all around the world came for inspiration, to meet the musicians, and to experience the unique environment of that time and place.

There were seven small apartments, quite cheap to rent, at 931 Royal. So whenever anyone new arrived in town, either to stay a few months or even to move here, we always recommended they move in whenever there was a vacancy. Quite often as soon as one couple moved out, another took their place. It sounded like a music school from morning till night with so many of us practicing on our horns or playing records.

Idolizing the musicians, we heard them every night at Preservation and Dixieland Halls. There were so many worth hearing in those days, players with strongly individual styles and personalities. Most had begun playing in the 1920s, and a few had begun long before that. The trumpeter Peter Bocage, for example, had been playing professionally since around 1906. Most of them were very friendly, and we were on a first-name basis with famous musicians like Punch Miller, Slow Drag Pavageau, Louis Nelson,

George Lewis, Kid Howard, Albert Burbank, Paul Barbarin . . . I
found it quite extraordinary.

One day before Christmas in 1966 the phone rang. It was Andrew Jefferson, snare drummer with the Olympia, on the line.

"I've got this gig on New Year's Eve. Can you play 'Auld Lang
Syne'?"

"Well, yeah, I guess so. What's up?"

"That's what you got to do—you got to play 'Auld Lang Syne' at
midnight. I'm goin' to get you, Tommy Sancton on clarinet, and
get Lars on guitar. My brother Tom's goin' to play piano."

"Thomas Jefferson on piano?"

"Yeah. He's OK."

And he was. And with his older brother in charge, the great
trumpet player hardly said a word all night, playing pretty fair
band piano. We played the tunes we knew in a large barroom for a
party of white folks, who danced and paid us little attention. Inex-
perienced as I was, when midnight rolled around I was so nervous
I almost forgot how to play *Auld Lang Syne*. It was my first New
Year's Eve gig. Why did Andrew hire us? I really don't know. Perhaps because we were friends?

Luckily, after my summer of travel I was reinstated in the Young
Tuxedo Brass Band, as well as continuing to fill in when needed
with the Olympia. Harold Dejan hired me to play the Zulu Parade
at Mardi Gras for three years in a row. We started at Shakespeare
Park uptown on the corner of Washington and Loyola at 8:30 in
the morning. I had to get a Freret bus which was not easy on Carnival morning. The first year I was five or ten minutes late and I
had to run to catch up with the band. "You're late!" said Harold.
"Don't make a habit of that or nobody's going to hire you again."
I learned my lesson. Another time, temperatures had dropped to
below freezing overnight and it never warmed up all day. There
was ice in the puddles on the roads well into the afternoon. That
was a hard year. "Here," said Andrew Jefferson, passing me a flask
of whisky. "Have some anti-freeze."

Dejan's Olympia Brass Band, Zulu parade, Mardi Gras, 1966. Photo: Jules Cahn, gifted by Cahn to Clive Wilson. Used by permission.

Parades and funerals maintained a sense of continuity with the traditions in the African American community. Even Thomas Jefferson, who worked six hours a night, six days a week, and had every reason to save his lip, would say: "You just got to do this to keep it going!" The money was low even by 1960s standards: parades paid $3.00 to $4.00 an hour per man, and funerals paid $6.50 no matter how long they lasted. That would depend on how many preachers were in the church. The low wage scale enabled the old organizations to continue hiring bands even as their membership dwindled.

Collecting brass band music became quite a passion with me. I remember the day I was playing a church parade in Algiers with the Young Tuxedo, and one of the church members, a Mrs. Smith, was pointed out to me as the lady who had reared Red Allen, his aunt. He always stayed with her when he visited New Orleans, though this was the summer of 1967, so Red had recently died. While I was talking to her, Mrs. Smith quite unexpectedly mentioned that she had all the Henry Allen Sr. Brass Band music (Red's

Peter Bocage, 1967. Photo: John Edser, used by permission.

father) and told me to come back in a couple of weeks to look at it. She gave it all away—some to Alvin Alcorn, who was planning to get his Imperial Brass Band together, some to Andrew Morgan, and some to me. It was a couple of boxes of faded yellowing music, incomplete, but enough to whet my appetite for more.

One musician with a large collection of music, neatly stored in filing cabinets, was trumpeter Peter Bocage. He showed it to me at his house in Algiers and talked proudly of the days when he played in the Superior Orchestra (he was the musical director), the A. J. Piron Orchestra, and the Excelsior Brass Band. All three were reading bands, and he had kept the arrangements. "These fellows today wouldn't know how to play this stuff," he said, echoing the old prejudice of the schooled musicians against those who read little or none at all.

In the early years of the twentieth century, the Masonic organizations often specified which marches they wanted, and the band was expected to play them as written. Many musicians I talked to remembered the Excelsior. As Earl Humphrey said: "You should have heard them; it was beautiful. They didn't play loud like the bands of today, but you could hear every instrument; they voiced so well together."

Bocage would not allow anyone to copy or acquire his arrangements, and when he died, neither would his family. Everyone from Percy Humphrey to the Jazz Archive tried to obtain the music, but the family was intractable. Perhaps they were ashamed of Bocage's life as a musician.

Harold Dejan, Kid Sheik, and Emanuel Sayles were among the first to invite us to accompany them on private jobs. I could sit behind the band most of the evening, and maybe sit in with them on the last set. I would watch and listen. Without knowing it, I had become an apprentice and was learning more than just music. I noticed how Dejan handled the people, how he would save certain tunes until they were requested, usually with a tip ("money numbers," he called them), and how he'd play soft, slow tunes near the end when people started to leave. Sometimes he'd get off early that way. On one occasion in 1965 he took Lars Edegran and myself to the South Siders Halloween Dance at the Autocrat Club, a private club. In those days, the musicians' union rules specified minimum numbers of musicians in the band, depending on the venue. With the Autocrat, the minimum was ten pieces. It was unusual for us to be able to hear an African American band play for dancing in an African American club. They featured swing standards as well as the usual New Orleans second line parade tunes.[1]

The Mardi Gras season is everyone's favorite time of year. Usually there would be two balls in the African American community each night of the week from Twelfth Night to Carnival Day. When Harold took me along to one of these balls, I was invited to sit with friends of his who had their own table, trestle tables covered with red and white-checkered cloth. Everyone brought their own food and drinks, and all they had to do was buy the set-up and buckets of ice from the establishment. It was like a picnic at night, with fried chicken, potato salad, devilled eggs, all you could eat. Dejan asked if I might sit in. Although this was a courtesy commonly extended on the last set, Percy Humphrey, who was the bandleader,[2] said it wouldn't look right as I wasn't wearing a suit. Dejan replied: "What's it matter, he looks like he has a suit on!" Percy gave in, of course.

At times some of the musicians would invite us to eat out at restaurants in their own neighborhoods, where we were introduced to the variety and delights of New Orleans Creole cuisine—okra gumbo, boiled shrimp or crawfish, boiled crabs, crawfish etouffé, shrimp creole. The most usual place for us to meet local musicians was at Buster's restaurant on the corner of Orleans and Burgundy Streets. By this time Buster had raised his prices, but not by much—a plate of red beans and rice had gone up to 27 cents. He added extra flavor by pouring all the fat from the fried or stewed chicken into the pot. This was a cheap, high-calorie meal for laborers and dockworkers. He served food all day, staying open as a barroom at night, all night on Saturday, and only closing as the sun came up on Sunday morning.

For something to eat late at night, you had to go to a restaurant across the street. Next to the barber shop on Burgundy Street was a hole-in-the-wall establishment called William's. Never mind the concrete floor and cinder block walls, with "Red" doing the cooking, they served the very best fried chicken in town, seasoned to perfection. The customers were friendly, if rough—it was not uncommon to find a drunk sleeping it off under your table—but they never bothered us. A fight broke out at the bar one night and one of the bodies came flying across the room, crashing into us. To this day I can hear Kid Sheik's laugh: "Heh, heh, heh!" and from Manny Sayles: "Look out there, Gates!" The situation evaporated as quickly as it had flared up. Often as not, it was in this type of environment that we heard personal stories from musicians like Sayles, Paul Barnes, Jim Robinson, Kid Sheik and Harold Dejan. Never in my wildest dreams did I imagine I would be living in a place like this.

Music was something we ate and slept with, always practicing, playing records, and talking about jazz. To the New Orleans musicians, who seemed to talk about everything under the sun *except* music, we must have seemed quite strange. Normal conversation for them revolved around food, cooking, women, fishing, or where to meet before the next gig. Nevertheless, we heard the occasional story about a deceased musician, or learned how he had played a certain tune. Paul "Polo" Barnes, a strict traditionalist, actually gave me a set of rules concerning the role of the trumpet:

"First you play the introduction loud, kind of loud, then soften up. Play the melody soft in the first chorus. The trumpet always plays the melody in the first and last chorus. The only difference is: you play the out-chorus with more drive." He added: "You can play a pick-up to your solo and always end it with a gap for the next fellow to play *his* pick-up." I'm afraid these simple rules have been forgotten today.

Imagine my delight one day, shortly after Manny Sayles had returned from Chicago, when Polo hired Trevor Richards and me to play with him on a private gig—a birthday party for some friends in his neighborhood. Sayles made up the quartet, and initially it seemed, Polo and Manny were mostly concerned about sharing the pitcher of beer equally between them.

"See, Manny," said Polo. "I'll just put the beer here between us, so you can see where it is. Just help yourself. OK?"

"OK, Gates," responded Sayles. Sayles called all musicians "Gates," which is short for Gatemouth, one of Louis Armstrong's nicknames.

Now Trevor and I were doing our best to follow Polo's rules—in Trevor's case, he played two-beat until the out-chorus when he switched to four-beat on the bass drum, coupled with what the old-timers call "Red Happy," an offbeat cymbal hit with snare drum fills. That's when we found out why Polo had hired us. He turned to Sayles with a big grin on his face: "See that, Manny, what did I tell you! They play just like us!"

A TALE OF PERCY HUMPHREY

Percy Humphrey was a trumpet man who enjoyed timing his notes with obvious care and thought, placing his uncomplicated phrases with poise and grace. He would play alternately softly and with warmth, growl fiercely with a plunger mute, or ride high above the band with his characteristic clear, wide-open tone.

Not often in the years that I heard him did Percy really open up on the trumpet as he would in his younger days. But I have seen him, when he was feeling good, stop by Preservation Hall after a private engagement, take out his horn in the back, and blow over and above the band from behind the audience! Just occasionally he liked to show off.

"Man, Percy is hell when he's drinking!" exclaimed Harold Dejan when I told him about it.

Another time in the late 1960s, Percy was the contractor for a Masonic lodge anniversary parade. There were three brass bands: the Olympia, the Young Tuxedo, and a pick-up band. Since Percy had stopped playing parades himself after a car accident the year before, he met us at the finish to pay off the bandleaders. At the end of the parade we were all to play the same number, "Joe Avery's Piece." As we turned the final corner, there was Percy, his trumpet pointed right at us. I remember him blowing across the open space, his tone and volume rising above and simply dominating all three bands. In everything, Percy understood timing. He knew when to pick his moment.

Alvin Alcorn, 1975. Photo: Clive Wilson collection.

A TALE OF ALVIN ALCORN

Alvin Alcorn took a keen interest in young aspiring musicians, and his home was open to all. He gave advice and trumpet lessons freely to all comers, whether New Orleanians or visitors, while his wife Lulsbia made sure they had a good plate of food inside them before they went on their way. To many of us, it was a home away from home. Alvin explained: "I have friends from all over the world, and many of them have visited me and my family. You see, I always try to reach the public when I'm playing."

Born September 7, 1912, Alvin no doubt had to be a musician. His older brother Oliver, a good reedman, used to rehearse with his friends around the house, and trumpeter George McCullum started to give young Alvin lessons. They quickly became great admirers of each other's playing. In fact, they were so close in style and temperament that Alvin was for many years thought to be related to McCullum.

Alvin advanced rapidly. "I started gigging around the city. I played with Armand Piron and with the Henry Allen Sr. and the Excelsior Brass Bands, passing for age. I went in the musicians' union when I was fifteen years old! That put me in a category where I could work with some of the finer musicians.

"My first job on the road was with Clarence Desdune's Joyland Revelers. McCullum was out on the road with this band and had come back from a leave of absence he had taken from his job as a cotton inspector. They sent for me on his recommendation and I joined the band in Omaha. They wouldn't let me into the club as I was too young. I told the doorman I was supposed to join the band. They called in the manager who finally said, 'If you're a New Orleans trumpeter, play "Panama."' I stepped back and gave him a little 'Panama' and he let me in. Little Brother Montgomery was on piano in that band."

After that first summer on the road, Alvin returned to New Orleans and began working with many groups including A. J. Piron and a year at a taxi dance hall with Captain John Handy's band, replacing trumpeter Lee Collins.

In 1932 Alvin went to San Antonio to join the Don Albert Band. They traveled all over the United States and recorded eight sides in 1936. It was a large swing band with four trumpets and, when Don Albert moved over to front the band, Alvin played first trumpet.

Returning to New Orleans in 1937, Alvin played the summer season on the steamer *President*, once again with Piron, then joined the Sidney Desvigne Orchestra that included sidemen Louis Cottrell, Louis Barbarin, Waldren "Frog" Joseph, and Louis Nelson. He stayed with them until after World War II.

Alvin began playing the Paddock Lounge on Bourbon Street for Papa Celestin in 1951, and it was through working with the Paddock band that Alvin met Kid Ory. "We went to the Beverly Cavern on the West Coast for a month, replacing Ory, who'd gone to San Francisco. Toward the end of our stay, Kid Ory came into the club and asked me to join his band right away. He'd asked me back during the War, but I couldn't go at that time because of the housing shortage."

Alvin was with Ory from 1954–58, making many recordings, a European tour, and an appearance in *The Benny Goodman Story*.

Back in New Orleans and constantly in demand, Alvin worked in succession with George Lewis (1958), Paul Barbarin (1959), Albert "Papa" French at Dixieland Hall (1962–64), George Lewis at Preservation Hall (1965–68), Louis Cottrell at Economy Hall, Crazy Shirley's, and Heritage Hall, and leading his own band. Besides numerous tours overseas, his trio was a longtime feature at the Commander's Palace Jazz Brunch.

Known for the beauty of his tone and for never missing or cracking a note, Alvin's uncomplicated, melodic way of swinging the lead was rooted in a solid technique and musical training. I began to see the need to begin addressing my own lack of technique, and so was fortunate to become Alvin's student. For a time, as I went through a period of imitating him, he called me "Junior." Back in 1967, he had even proposed I run for the board of the black musicians' union local, which I politely turned down as I felt it was inappropriate.

Alvin grew up in a time when sight reading and good intonation were essential. He made me listen to myself with a more critical ear, made me aware that I could choose what sound I wanted, had me practice without a vibrato so that I could control it musically, and choose when to sustain a note or cut it short. This was enormously influential in the eventual development of my own style and self-expression. Later when taking "legit" lessons from a symphony player, I was able to understand the teaching that Alvin had begun.

Some years later I recorded Alvin Alcorn for my record label, New Orleans Records, in Lu and Charlie's, a local club, which turned out to be the first recording to be issued under his own name. The trio sides include a haunting blues tune that Alvin had recorded back in the 1930s with Don Albert's big band, "Deep Blue Melody." I persuaded the *New Orleans Times-Picayune* to do a feature article about Alvin. In fact, a department of the paper fully intended to do a series of such features on a regular basis, but what has become popular today was considered of little interest then. A senior editor vetoed the project. "Our readers aren't interested in jazz musicians," he said. Times have changed.

Despite the apparently "straight" elements in Alcorn's method, he played with a distinct rhythm that was initially quite foreign to me. For a short time in the late 1970s I played with Alcorn's Imperial Brass Band, a revival of the name used by the legendary cornetist Manny Perez. Playing alongside Alvin and Sam Alcorn, father and son, I noticed that they played the melody and harmony with an identical rhythmic inflection. They began each phrase slightly ahead of the beat, then seemed to fall behind, and ended the phrase slightly ahead. At that time I found it impossible to duplicate. While I can demonstrate it today, it will never be quite the same—a bit like a Londoner mimicking a Yorkshire accent, I suppose.

A TALE OF MANUEL MANETTA

"You've got to meet my uncle Manuel," Freddie Kohlman told me one day. "Take the ferry to Algiers and I'll pick you up there."

The ferry goes from the foot of Canal Street and, to this day, it's the best way to ride on the Mississippi and view the New Orleans skyline, which in those days did not include any skyscrapers. Algiers Point, at a sharp bend in the river, is directly across from the French Quarter, but remains a quiet, old-fashioned residential community quite unlike the business district of New Orleans. Recently returned from Chicago where we had met at Jazz Limited, Freddie Kohlman was now playing six nights a week at the Paddock Lounge with Thomas Jefferson on trumpet.

True to his word, Freddie was waiting for me in his car, and we drove the short distance to Manetta's home. I knew a little about Manetta, but learned that he was born in 1889, began playing professionally in 1904, and was soon versatile enough, along with Tony Jackson, Frank Amaker, and Jelly Roll Morton, to play piano in Storyville, the district set aside for legal prostitution. Since those early days, he had mastered many instruments, played in many bands, and become the most renowned music teacher in New Orleans. He was also a marvelous raconteur and it took very little prompting by Freddie to get him started. Freddie just loved to hear him talk of those days back at the beginning of the twentieth century, and I was simply spellbound.

Among the stories he told was one of catching the Algiers ferry (on the Algiers side) on a summer's evening, and being able to hear the sound of Buddy Bolden's horn drifting across the river from the Globe Theater near where Armstrong Park is today (previously Congo Square), a distance of about one mile. His idol was the pianist Tony Jackson, whose most famous composition is "Pretty Baby," and he considered him "the greatest single-handed entertainer in the world." Manetta told us of a short visit he made to Chicago in 1913. His gig was cancelled, but he felt the whole trip was worthwhile, nevertheless, because he was able to go to the club where Jackson, who had moved there the year before, was playing. Manetta was mesmerized all night.

The following year I unexpectedly had the opportunity to hear Manetta play. It was at the annual Creole Spring Fiesta Association Ball, which was held in May that year after their annual parade at the Corpus Christi School Hall.

The music was supplied by the Adams Family Band, which at these functions consisted of Dolly Adams (née Douroux), piano; two of her sons, Justin Adams, amplified guitar, and Gerald Adams, string bass; Alvin Alcorn, trumpet; and Alex Bigard, drums. In earlier years, the band consisted entirely of members of the Adams family. Gerald

Adams told me that once when they played for a dance in the country town of Westwego on the West Bank, a lady asked, in typical Westwego speech:

"Are y'all some kind of relate? I tell my husband: y'all look so much t'gedder, I cain't hardly tell ya alike!"

A few of us Europeans, invited to attend the ball by the bassist August Lanoix, who was an officer in the organization, sat behind the band until the last set when we were permitted to sit in. I vividly remember August beaming proudly as he danced by the band with his wife, exclaiming: "We've been married fifty years!"

Then seventy-eight years old and retired, Manetta was also Dolly's uncle and the Adams brothers' great-uncle. His playing left such an impression on me.

The band began shortly after 6:00 p.m. and everyone sounded wonderful. Dolly Adams played the first few numbers on piano while Manetta sat out. I was impressed with her drive and chording, although she said she had not recovered entirely from the stroke that affected her hands.

After a few numbers, Manetta took over on the piano for about an hour. Incorporating more variety than Dolly Adams and even more swing and drive, his playing was extraordinary. His left-hand bass figures, one of which was a walking boogie-woogie, changed every two choruses. Each change in the bass figure produced a subtle shift in the rhythm of the whole band. His right hand played ceaseless, flowery embellishments on some choruses, and syncopated chords like Dolly Adams on other choruses. I was reminded of James P. Johnson's piano playing on "Wild Cat Blues," with Sidney Bechet, from the *This Is Jazz* radio broadcast.

On the out choruses the rhythm section would really bear down on the beat, providing, it seemed, the maximum drive possible. Trevor Richards told me Bigard was playing these out choruses in the style of James "Red Happy" Bolton from around 1920 and before. He was shown this style by Cie Frazier. It was a combination of offbeats on the cymbal, and snare drum work between the offbeats. Manetta shifted, for the first time in the tune, to an energetic 4/4 beat with both hands. You can get a good idea of the effect this created by listening to the out choruses of "Cake Walking Babies from Home," recorded in 1925 by the Clarence Williams Blue Five.

Later in the evening, Manetta played four or five numbers on the trumpet and trombone at the same time; a couple of waltzes, one of which was "The Waltz You Saved for Me," and simple tunes like "The Saints." The trombone was tied around his neck with a saxophone strap so that the mouthpiece rested on his lip and he could move the slide with his left hand. This provided a simple harmony part or vamp to the trumpet, held in the right hand, which carried the melody. Sometimes, with the same tremendous enthusiasm he had displayed on the piano, he played a riff in close harmony, sounding like a one-man brass section.

A TALE OF EMILE BARNES

According to Kid Howard, *the* clarinet player back in the 1920s was Emile Barnes, Paul's older brother. Everyone called him 'Mile (pronounced Meely). As he had suffered a couple of strokes in recent years, the only way we could hear him play was to visit him at home. Despite his wife's concern over his health, he loved to bring out his clarinet and play a few numbers with us on his front porch. 'Mile lived in a poor neighborhood next to the Desire Housing Project, so he always made sure we left before dark. English clarinetist Dick Cook, the only one among us who had a car in those days, drove out to see 'Mile more often and borrowed his clarinet to get it completely overhauled. When he returned it after several weeks without the rubber bands and leaking pads, 'Mile was quite overcome. As Dick told us: "He just held it in his hands like a kid with a new toy."

Emile Barnes, 1968. Photo: John Edser,
used by permission.

John Edser, Clive Wilson, Orange Kellin, Emile Barnes, Barnes's wife, Trevor Richards,
Dick Edser, Lars Edegran, and Tommy Sancton in doorway, 1968. Photo by Dick Cook,
owned by John Edser, used by permission.

Naturally we were eager to hear 'Mile with his renovated clarinet, and so piled into Dick Cook's car the very next weekend. It was well worth it. 'Mile was a different player without the squeaks. His long flowing lines, perfectly contrasting the melody, were quite new to me and unlike his recordings, though his throbbing, Sidney Bechet–like vibrato remained. We were treated to a glimpse of what he could do in his younger days.

Unfortunately, the experience gave 'Mile such a bad, restless night that his wife, sensibly, requested an end to the sessions. It was the last time I heard him play.

On Sunday afternoons during the summer and early autumn months, if there was no parade, we were often invited to back-yard parties organized by musicians and their families. Making me feel welcome, Harold Dejan even invited me to Christmas dinner at his home on my first year in New Orleans. Typically, Harold would drive us over to Kid Sheik's cousin's house or Booker T's house ("Booker T" Glass was the bass drummer in the Olympia Brass Band). Those of us in the foreign contingent made an instant warm-up band and, as the day wore on, many New Orleans musicians would come by and play; musicians such as Andrew Morgan, Earl Humphrey, Capt. John, Sylvester and Julius Handy, Milford Dolliole, Emanuel Sayles, Andrew Jefferson, Emanuel Paul, Ernest Roubleau, Chester Jones, Kid Sheik, Louis Nelson, Chester Zardis, and many more. Increasingly, the musical community and their fans seemed to make up a big family. Those long-ago days in the 1960s often feel like yesterday—red beans and rice and potato sal-ad in the kitchen, a bathtub full of ice to keep the beer and soft drinks cold, and dancing in the yard. Beyond that the details are blurred. One time after a rain, some old carpeting was put down over the muddy grass for the dancers. Another time, at Louis

Tony Fougerat at Audubon Park, 1967. Photo: Courtesy of GHB/Jazzology Records.

James's house, we ate a cowan (turtle, pronounced cow-wane) stew that was as highly seasoned as a Madras curry. Everyone packed up and went home when the sun went down.

And so, as it turned out, the majority of musicians I was listening to, and getting to know personally, were African American. I wanted to play like them, with a warm, relaxed swing, and a poignant quality of sound that I associate with the blues. It was the choice I made as I sensed a primary quality, an authority—unmistakable in Louis Armstrong or Sidney Bechet—in their music. In any case, when I listened to white musicians, I noticed that they, too, were influenced by African American musicians. One of the best white trumpet players to ever come out of New Orleans was Sharkey Bonano. I loved his sound, his swing, and flowing, yet "down-home" ideas. "Man, you know where that come from?" said Harold Dejan to me one day: "Kid Rena! (pronounced "Renay," as in French: "René"). When Sharkey was starting out he followed him all over town. He plays some of Rena's licks today."

Another white cornetist who listened to Kid Rena in his youth was Tony Fougerat. "He played a picnic every Sunday out at Milneberg" (pronounced Milenburg in New Orleans). Tony had picked me up to drive around town and talk about his life, and along the way giving me some advice. We went to his barbershop and as he sat in the chair he continued to talk about the cornet players he loved to hear. "I heard Emmett Hardy on the S.S. *Sidney*. The most outstanding were Louis Armstrong, Kid Rena, and Emmett Hardy. Though some of the others were good, too—Buddy Petit, Sam Morgan, Bunk Johnson, and Claiborne Williams. But for living in New Orleans, Kid Rena was about the best around." Interestingly, Emmett Hardy was the only white cornetist in the bunch.

"You know," he continued as the barber tidied up, "the Negro musicians play great, but we don't mix with them. We stay separate."

"I don't see why we have to do that today," I rejoined. Tony dropped the subject. With no hatred in him, it was simply that he had grown up in a segregated world. Seeing me live and associate with African Americans was quite incomprehensible to him. Yet a few years later, as he became more accustomed to desegregation, I saw him playing alongside them in Andrew Hall's Society Jazz Band at the Maple Leaf Bar every Friday.

But are African American musicians superior? A difficult area to discuss, of course; so, yes and no, in my opinion. From my perspective, only a very few people of any generation and from *any* ethnic group are driven to become musicians. And in a place like New Orleans, there have always been musicians of different abilities living and playing side by side. Whoever has the contact to get the gig is leader, and so everyone finds some work. Although there are great, average, and mediocre musicians among all ethnic groups and backgrounds, the original innovators of jazz, in my opinion, were a small group of talented African Americans from the Protestant, English-speaking, American sector of town. I've heard this from black, white, and Creole musicians, and it was immediately recognized as something quite new by everyone when they first heard it. Subsequently as they learned to play in that way, talented musicians from every background had a hand in its development. Yet I will add that, with the African American musicians who could play well, their music was more compelling, with an inner strength and emotional conviction—and *that* attracted me. Seemingly, there is an element from another dimension that I cannot find the words to describe.

I liked to sit with Tom Albert, an old Creole, on the stoop in front of his house on Burgundy Street and ask him questions about his early years. A cornet player, long since retired, Tom told me about the first time he heard Buddy Bolden's band around 1904, credited by their contemporaries to be the first band to play jazz. He was amazed: "I stood there with my mouth open so long, it got full of dirt!" Yet according to Kid Sheik, Tom Albert never learned to play jazz himself. But he remembered learning to play by ear. "What you goin' to do?" He explained. "You playin' a picnic with the music, see, and the sun goes down. There's no more light, so you just go on and play without it."

Peter Bocage said, when interviewed at Tulane:[3] "[Bolden and his band] made their own music and they played it their own way. So that's the way jazz started—just his improvisation." He continued: "Now this jazz business—I didn't start to playing that until I got mixed up with Bunk [Johnson] and them fellows . . . and that came right after Bolden" [i.e., 1907 or 1908].

The jazz drummer Tony Schreiner, one of the few white musicians seemingly without prejudice in New Orleans, told me about listening to bands at Milneburg on Lake Pontchartrain: "All of us played out there, in different camps [a camp is a house or shack built on pilings over the water], you know, and we'd hear a colored band across the water at the next camp. I tell you, there was something in their rhythm we could never quite get. It was a joy to hear them."

So like Tony, I wanted to sound like an African American musician, even if I only became mediocre. Today, I don't think along those lines. You can hear musicians from all backgrounds who are great, average, and mediocre. The ones I enjoy listening to are those that play from the heart, that play from that inner dimension as yet undefined. Should we call that "soul"?

SATURDAY NIGHT

Dancing has been popular in New Orleans from the very beginning of its history, and in the city and small towns across the river there were many dance halls for the locals. Bands played the popular songs of the day in a New Orleans jazz style, interspersed with waltzes and the occasional traditional jazz standard. But during the 1950s the number of dance halls dwindled with the changing times, and by the mid-sixties regular work in the dance halls was almost over. Just a few weekend spots remained. So for us newcomers to the city, Saturday night was a change of pace. It gave us an opportunity to see and experience New Orleans musicians playing for the locals away from the tourist world of the French Quarter.

The customers were white folks in their sixties, seventies, and eighties, as were the bands most of the time. While the music was usually unremarkable, we always had fun and enjoyed the casual atmosphere.

Occasionally an African American group would find work in a dance hall, as when Harold Dejan and Kid Sheik played a month of weekends at Springer's Bar. Dick Allen told me that Herb Morand and Albert Burbank used to play there in 1949 and 1950. Standing on the corner of Tchoupitoulas and Napoleon, the place is well known today. It was remodeled in the 1970s and named Tipitina's in honor of the famous song by R&B piano playing legend Professor Longhair.

Luthjen's, known as "The Old Folks Home," on Chartres and Marigny Streets below[1] Elysian Fields, was an easy walk from the French Quarter, so we'd often end up there late on Saturday nights as the band was hired until two in the morning. The quartet of African American musicians[2] lost the job in 1965, but moved over to the Harmony Inn where they were not treated well. Feeling uncomfortable about this, I only made one visit and did not return. The band quit after a few months.

The replacement in Luthjen's was a somewhat uninspired white group. The clarinetist Luke Schiro enjoyed talking to us "outsiders," and when the owner found out some of us were British (he was stationed there in World War II), he made us feel quite welcome. However, one of our group was not allowed in when he showed up with a camera. Cameras were not permitted because, according to Luke, some of the patrons, in their sixties and seventies no less, were on a date with someone else's wife or husband!

To take the Saturday night cruise on the S.S. *President*, a side-wheel paddle steamer, was to step out of the present into a world where time seemingly had stood still for thirty or forty years. The old dance floor was beginning to buckle in places and the only cooling in the summertime came from breezes off the river. To be heard from the balcony, the music had to penetrate, as if through a fog, the incessant whirring of the ceiling fans, the echoing sounds of the customers, and the distant throb of the steam engines.

The Crawford-Ferguson Night Owls were required to play three dances every fifteen minutes. Though not as strictly monitored by Captain Streckfus as in the old days, the sets were numbered and displayed on a board next to the band. With an eight-piece union minimum on the *President*, the band used both banjo and guitar, and accordion in place of piano. Strange as that might sound, the lady accordionist, Joel Buck, had a good sense of swing and, with Chink Martin Sr. (of the New Orleans Rhythm Kings fame) playing the string bass, how could she go wrong?[3] Hank Kmen, who played reeds, had a dry, deadpan wit. I remember him, one Saturday

night, crooning the modified words to a popular song as the dancers, unheeding, shuffled around the floor: "I'm dancing with tears
in my eyes / 'cause the girl in my arms is a boy."

If you took the Magazine Street bus up to Lyons and walked two
blocks toward the river, there in a neighborhood above[4] the Irish
Channel,[5] you'd find Munster's Bar. I suppose it was my favorite
place for a Saturday night out, both for the music and its unusual run-down, informal character. Most of the band, led by Tony
Fougerat, came from the same section of town. The place looked
a little rough but nobody ever got out of line. Mrs. Trapani saw to
that. Looking like a bouncer, she simply dwarfed everyone else. As
the only young people, we were conspicuous, but once Mrs. Trapani discovered that we were musicians, she made sure nothing
happened to us. Her husband Joe often sat in on clarinet and tenor
sax, and their son Frank played lead trumpet in the Blue Room
Orchestra at the Roosevelt Hotel.

The musicians referred to Munster's as "The House of Shock"
since so many of the patrons could well have stepped out of that
section of a wax museum! A more peculiar, craggy-looking bunch
you could not find. The band did not disappoint in that regard
either, for besides the one-armed, left-handed trombone player
Joseph "Red" Margiotta, they had a legless guitar player and, on
one occasion, a drummer with clubbed feet and hands who held
the sticks between the stubs of his fingers with elastic bands. But
the band had a good "rap," as they say in New Orleans (meaning a
strong beat), and Fougerat played a Conn Victor cornet in a "ratty"
old-fashioned style. Quickly becoming a good friend, Tony would
invite us youngsters to sit in with the band, and I learned quite a
few old pop songs from him.

I was able to record the band for record producer George Buck
on Al Rose's covered back porch, which had ideal acoustics. "The
Fouge" (as Tony was known)[6] decided to call it *Every Man a King*,
which was the theme song of Huey P. Long, the governor of Louisiana during the Great Depression. Joe Trapani played both clarinet

and tenor sax, so Al Rose, a self-appointed expert on the music, made sure he himself was not present to hear such a "dreadful band" (his words). Al had discovered an article that claimed Adolph Sax invented the saxophone as a cure for asthma! Well, although truth is often stranger than fiction, I'm not convinced about that one! In any case, as Al Rose did not suffer from asthma, he saw no reason to be seen in the same room with one.

"The only restaurant in New Orleans featuring Dixie Land Jazz and serving famous New Orleans seafood," said the menu at The Old Fisherman's Wharf. For six weeks in the fall of 1967 in the old resort of West End on Lake Pontchartrain, you could hear John Henry McNeil's Crescent City Crystals[7] each Friday and Saturday night. Built on pilings over Lake Pontchartrain, Fisherman's Wharf cleared away enough tables to create a dance floor in front of the band. As none of us had our own transportation in those days, we were able to get out there only a couple of times. McNeil, also the leader of the Apollo Brass Band, humorously referred to himself as "Black Irish." The opportunity to hear his interesting group elsewhere was simply nonexistent.

For a brief period of four or five weekends in May 1966, Kid Thomas was hired back to play for dancing on Saturday nights at the Old Fireman's Hall in Westwego. The crowd was more the type you would expect to see at a country and western place, and many of them remembered "Tom" (as they called him), for he had played dance halls on the West Bank of the river most of his life. He brought out his old sign again that simply read "Kid Thomas Dixieland Band."[8] Quite a distance outside New Orleans, the hall drew people from the surrounding country to pass a good time eating and drinking on the trestle tables which were set up around the dance floor—and dancing was popular. It was a lovely experience for us to hear Kid Thomas, for probably the last time, play in such an unpretentious setting. The music was refreshingly mellow and relaxed.

A couple of years later, I collaborated in a recording of Kid Thomas with another British visitor, Richard Ekins—promptly dubbed "Lord Richard" by Kid Thomas's bass player Joe Butler on account of his long wavy blond hair, which resembled pictures of Jesus. We felt it important to use an old dance hall in Kid Thomas's own neighborhood of old Algiers, selecting Kohlman's Tavern, owned by Freddie Kohlman's father Louis. After hearing the band play for dancing in Westwego, we had a pretty clear idea of the music we wanted to document. The recording went beautifully, featuring some lovely complementary playing between Louis Nelson on trombone and Charlie Hamilton on piano.

I remember an occasion when Trevor Richards and I went to visit Kid Thomas's drummer Sammy Penn. Trevor had just repaired his snare drum for the umpteenth time and was returning it. At this stage of Sammy's life, his drinking had begun to catch up with him and he told us his doctor had forbidden him whisky. "But he didn't say anything about gin!" he added gleefully. As I remember, he had begun to speed up when drinking, so it was really important to keep Sammy and booze apart at the recording session. We almost succeeded.

Acting as a producer can be a bit of a balancing act between giving input and keeping out of the way. But getting the very best of Kid Thomas's blues playing took a little bit of suggestion. The first two takes of a blues were generally pretty good but unremarkable. Tom Bethell, who was also present listening to the session, reminded me of a blues Thomas occasionally played. So we asked him to do it again, but this time slower and in the key of C, and would he please take four choruses in? He looked quizzically at us for a moment, then seemed to understand and said OK. Like most of the New Orleans musicians, he was always kind and generous with his fans. Bethell's instinct turned out to be correct. This blues began as a moan, and ended in a roar! The highlight of the recording, we were practically blown over by the force of his out choruses. When it was over, Louis Nelson, originally rather skeptical of our ability to produce anything at all, gave his stamp of approval. As he walked out of the door, he simply said: "Good session, boy!" Coming from a man of few words, it meant a lot.

Even though this setting was fast becoming anachronistic, the dance halls and the music felt timeless, and I could easily visualize what it must have been like to go dancing on the Lakefront, on a riverboat, or at a country town like Westwego, in days gone by.

A couple of years later, inspired by several sips of ouzo in Johnny White's Bar across from Preservation Hall, a record collector friend of mine, Paige Van Vorst, and I had the bright idea to start a record label of our own. To this day, I can remember the smile spreading over Paige's Tweedledum-like face as he sipped a glass of ouzo for the first time. "Tell you what," he exclaimed, "Let's make ouzo the official drink of the record company!" and promptly slipped and fell backwards onto the floor. Still laughing, he got up, apparently unhurt, all excited about our new venture.

We began by buying enough of the takes for an LP of the *Kid Thomas at Kohlman's Tavern* session, which had originally been issued in Britain by Lord Richard. Mike Casimir designed the front cover, using a high contrast print of Michael Smith's black and white photo of Kid Thomas's face. When Barbara Reid saw the cover, she was amazed at the likeness to an old wooden carving she had of Papa Legba who, in West African tradition, is the trickster figure, roughly equivalent to Hermes or Mercury, the go-between god of communication. I'm sure that had something to do with the record sales!

PLANNING MY RETURN
TO BRITAIN

Although my original plan was to live in New Orleans for two years, I was now into my third year and loving every minute of it. Yet I wondered: what would it be like to return to Britain as someone with this unusual and often amazing experience behind me? So I decided to return in the summer. Having saved up from my day job, I could afford to quit at the bank and enjoy some free time.

The first thing I did was revisit all the musicians I'd met in Connecticut a couple of years before. I tagged along with a carload of friends I'd met in New Orleans, who took me as far as Washington, D.C., where I spent a week researching brass band arrangements in the Library of Congress. All I can remember of the trip is that our driver claimed to be a retired warlock and had a love of setting off fireworks—really loud ones. I had no idea what to make of him, but once in Connecticut, I was lucky to be able to stay with Dick and Sandra Cook, an English couple I'd met in New Orleans who had lived in one of the apartments at 931 Royal Street. Dick was playing clarinet with the local jazz band.

I was looking forward to a short tour the Connecticut Jazz Club had organized for Kid Sheik's band with Capt. John Handy on the alto sax. Handy was as hot as ever, and the five musicians from New Orleans[1] were augmented by a couple of the locals. RCA Victor decided to record the band under Handy's name while they were in the area, which gave Handy something of a shock. He wanted to record, not with Kid Sheik's band, but with New York

swing musicians as he had done the year before. But RCA insisted they wanted him to record with a New Orleans band. Handy
agreed if they could add Buck Clayton on trumpet—having heard
him on a record with Sidney Bechet, he really liked his playing. I
knew nothing of this, but one day Fred Paquette, who seemed to
be negotiating these arrangements, came to me and told me what
was going on.

"Handy wants a stronger trumpet section, and he's asking for
Buck Clayton," he announced. "If we can't get Clayton, would you
play instead?"

I nearly fell off my chair in surprise.

"Get Buck Clayton," I replied. "He'd be great with Handy."

"But he's not answering the phone; we think he must be out of
town. Handy doesn't want Sheik, not on his own at any rate. We
can't leave him out now he's here, and you've played with him a lot.
You'd fit in."

"I'll only do it if you can't get whoever Handy wants, and if
Handy agrees," I said. But I was thinking the session wasn't what
Handy wanted anyway, and would not be a full band of New Orleans musicians in any case. The quality of the session was so compromised that I might as well play on it and get the experience.

And so it was—three days in the famous RCA Victor studio with
some of the greats. Jack Bradley, whom I'd met at the Metropole in
1964, was the photographer, and Herbie Friedwald, who had recorded those wonderful sessions in New Orleans for Riverside Records, came to listen.

"I've never heard a young white guy with Peter Bocage's tone
before," he said.

"Thanks, but I'm really trying to play like Kid Howard."

"Oh, yeah? But you have Peter's tone."

At the end of the third day I turned to the bassist Chester Zardis
and said: "Whew! That was tiring."

He smiled: "Well, now you know what's involved."

Trevor Richards, Clayton Duerr, Dick Cook, Clive Wilson, at the El Morocco, 1968.
Photo: Clive Wilson collection.

Dick and Sandra Cook had also decided it was time to return to Britain for a while, but wanted to spend a few more months in New Orleans before doing so. The three of us set off in Dick's old Ford, stopping off with friends of mine in Alexandria, just outside Washington, D.C. This was in the week after Martin Luther King was assassinated, so there was a curfew at night in all the cities. We traveled by day, and stayed another night at George Buck's place outside Atlanta before returning to New Orleans. Trevor Richards had found an unbelievably cheap place to rent on the corner of Governor Nicholls and Decatur Streets—just seventy-five dollars a month, which we shared. Situated in a quiet, out-of-the-way part of the French Quarter, the flat roof above the third floor overlooked the warehouses next to the Farmer's Market and the Mississippi. All the stores in the neighborhood catered to the local residents and the longshoremen who worked on the docks. I remember a fish market, and a grocery store that was open twenty-four hours a day.

For a brief time we lived a carefree, bohemian lifestyle, listening to jazz and sitting in with the Olympia Brass Band whenever they played a parade. When we played as a group for one of the regular New Orleans Jazz Club evenings, Joe Gemelli, the MC, announced that we had all come from England and Sweden. I jokingly told the audience we needed some work to make enough money to pay for our trip home, which brought a laugh. But the next day Joe Gemelli called. "Go down to the El Morocco," he announced. "They're looking for a band to play six nights a week."

The El Morocco, in the 200 block of Bourbon Street, is where the George Lewis band had played in the early 1950s, but had not featured music for many years. So clearly Gemelli had some clout with the local powers that be. We got the gig, Trevor, Dick, and I, and hired an old guitar player named "Sunshine" (Clayton Duerr) to play with us. Six hours a night is hard work, but we were young. The club was mostly empty, however, and they made little effort to attract customers. An old craggy-looking cop was the one regular every night, who seemed to think his job was to keep out anyone he didn't like the look of. They asked us to stay on, but after three weeks of the grind, both Trevor and Dick were ready to book their trip home. I planned to leave a couple of months later in any case, so we gave them our notice.

I registered with the Scandinavian shipping office up on Magazine Street, and a few weeks later got the call to work my passage back on a Norwegian freighter that was bound for Rotterdam. As the boat pulled out from the Poydras Street Wharf, a small entourage came to wish me goodbye. Lars "Sumpen" Sundbom played "Just a Closer Walk with Thee," the sound of his cornet floating across the water.

I had been in touch with Mike Casimir in London, letting him know my arrival date. I took the boat train from Rotterdam and he was kind enough to meet me at Liverpool Street Station at seven in the morning.

"Welcome home," he said. "God, I didn't know your trunk would be *this* heavy!" as we loaded it into the back of his station wagon. "We'll get rid of this, have some breakfast, and head over to the pick-up."

"Pick-up? What pick-up?"

"Oh, didn't I tell you? We're playing a carnival with the brass band and meeting everyone in the pub at Notting Hill Gate at eleven. I hope you have your parade cap."

We had to wait a few minutes extra in the pub for everyone to show up.

"How come you're late?" said Mike to the late arrivals. "This man came all the way from New Orleans and *he's* on time!"

ON THE ROAD

The Olympia Brass Band was to play a trade show in Berlin that August 1968, and Harold Dejan invited Trevor Richards, Dick Cook, and myself to come over and play with him, since we had all just moved back to Britain (Dick and Sandra came over on their honeymoon). Through Trevor's contacts in Germany, I met up with trombonist Frank Naundorf, who arranged several extra gigs for the Olympia and hired us to play with his band, the White Eagle. After playing a month with them and recording with the Olympia in that exciting city that never seemed to slow down day or night, I returned to Britain. Within a week or so, Barry Martyn asked me to join his band.

Besides playing with the Young Tuxedo Brass Band in New Orleans, I had never played on a regular basis in a professional band, and was keenly aware that I needed that experience. In my first few weeks back, I sat in with several groups in local pubs and found it quite difficult. Rhythmically, they were different from New Orleans bands, and it threw me off. I had learned to fit my playing around a typical New Orleans two-beat, and British bands seemed to have an intense four-beat. Simply put, I did not have enough technique to adapt. Playing in my own self-taught way had become an obvious handicap. So I began taking lessons from Phil Parker in London, who was very kind and encouraging. I went through a slow process of unlearning everything I had picked up on my own and replacing that with the basics of a good technique. Just to break myself of the worst of my bad habits took eighteen months. Later, I took private lessons in the rudiments of music to get a better understanding of what it was all about from a theoretical standpoint. Because of my practical experience in New Orleans, I was able to immediately benefit from this.

Although the Barry Martyn band had a good reputation for playing in the New Orleans style, times were tough for traditional jazz in Britain. The "Trad Boom" of the late 1950s and early 1960s had faded away with the rise in popularity of the Beatles and the Rolling Stones. Money was low after the expense of maintaining our bandwagon, so I had to continue living as cheaply as possible and subsidized my income from my savings. In fact, the bandwagon broke down on the way home from my first gig, an omen of difficult times ahead. We had to push it to the nearest garage in the middle of the night. Thank God it wasn't raining! But in spite of the many frustrations, I was happy living the life I chose. With weekly rehearsals, we learned new tunes and worked out some simple arrangements. It was just the experience I needed. Both our clarinetist Dick Douthwaite and I had lived in New Orleans, so we began to play a little less like an English band and a little more like a New Orleans band. But faced with the problems of changing my trumpet method, I was not playing particularly well when I joined the band. Unfortunately, for whatever reason, there was frequent tension and arguing between us. In fact, I have never known another band that argued so much. But by living through that time together we forged lifelong friendships and had some good times.

On the positive side, we rehearsed tunes we had never played before, tunes that had been recorded in the 1920s by bands such as those of A. J. Piron, Sam Morgan, and Lee Collins, broadening our repertoire considerably. Memorizing much of what we played from the original recordings, we were still basically on the outside of the music looking in. Nevertheless, it was good practice, and I got to feel what those musicians were doing musically, and what a band can do to sound good together. Perhaps I was approaching the inside of the music by slow degrees.

Several New Orleans musicians toured with us—Kid Sheik, Andrew Morgan, Emanuel Sayles, and Alton Purnell—and I enjoyed every moment with them. With Morgan, we resurrected several tunes from the Sam Morgan repertoire, his brother's band that Andrew had played with in the 1920s. With Sayles, we played a few tunes he had recorded with Lee Collins back in 1929, and he amazed us by playing the same wonderful banjo solos as on the original. And Purnell was the pianist on that first jazz recording I ever heard when I was thirteen—"Tishomingo Blues" with Bunk Johnson—becoming George Lewis's regular pianist. As he had moved to Los Angeles in the late 1950s, we had never met.

"How long did you say you lived in New Orleans?" he asked me one night.

"Three years."

"You sound pretty good," he continued. "Why don't you go back for three more years and become a *real* trumpet player?" I gave it some thought, increasingly, as time went on.

I maintained a New Orleans connection also by continuing to play with Mike Casimir's Paragon Brass Band. Seven out of ten members of the band had been on extended visits to New Orleans, so we knew what we wanted to sound like. But I found the band to be quite weak compared to those in New Orleans, so we began rehearsing and discussing the role of each of the instruments. What an improvement that made! It was all quite simple when we thought about it, and everyone was pleased with the result. We were learning the ropes little by little.

Each summer, the Martyn band traveled for a couple of months in the States, playing in New England, New Orleans, and St. Paul, Minnesota, at the Hall Brothers' Emporium of Jazz. The time in New Orleans allowed us to renew a connection with the source of our inspiration, spending time with the musicians who had become our friends.

The highlight of our trip in 1970 was playing at the "Hello Louis" concert in the Shrine Auditorium, Los Angeles, to celebrate Armstrong's seventieth birthday. Our tour in the States was operating on a shoestring, but we made it somehow, driving from New England to Los Angeles in three days, stopping only twice just long enough to sleep.

When we arrived we had a night to recover, then played a short set as a warm-up band in the raised orchestra pit. It was a compromise; the musicians' union would not allow us to perform on stage as an official part of the concert. Although we were nervous at first with six thousand people in the audience, everyone seemed to enjoy us. Imagine our surprise, though, when we were asked to go back on because Sarah Vaughan, the opening act, was late. Would we play until she arrived? By this time, all nervousness had evaporated, and we received a standing ovation!

The rest of the evening was simply brilliant. The curtain opened on a giant rocking chair. Hoagy Carmichael, the MC, brought Louis Armstrong out from the wings and sat him down. Together they sang Hoagy's composition "Rockin' Chair," which they had recorded some forty years before. I still have chills going down my spine whenever I remember it.

These trips to New Orleans each summer made me realize how much I missed the city and the easy living I remembered. I was increasingly homesick for that distant place in my life, a place that I recognized had become a part of me. In any case, paying the bills by playing traditional jazz in Britain was an uphill struggle. So I gave my notice and left the band in Massachusetts at the end of the tour. Arranging for a friend in London to ship my few belongings, I made my way back to New Orleans. But that was an ongoing adventure. On previous trips through New York I had heard the Newport Jazz Festival All-Stars with trumpeter Buck Clayton, clarinetist Pee Wee Russell, trombonist J. C. Higginbotham, and George Wein on piano. Higgy's feature was a rubato version of "Dear Old Southland." This time, friends in Boston took me on an hour's drive north to Lenny's on the Turnpike, where I heard the great Count Basie Band in an informal club much like Preservation Hall, only larger. I spent a few more days in New York, staying in Greenwich Village with Hank O'Neil, the producer of Chiaroscuro Records. I heard trumpeter Charlie Shavers at the Metropole, who had taken over the spot after Red Allen passed away, and participated in an avant garde recording by composer John Cage (my job was to slam a door at certain times in the performance).

Passing once again through New York, I heard a band called the Saints and Sinners that played for dinner and dancing. Led by pianist Charles "Red" Richards, it included Herman Autrey, trumpet; Herb Hall, clarinet; George "Buddy" Tate, tenor sax; and bass and drums. Trombonist Vic Dickenson was originally co-leader, but had recently left to join the World's Greatest Jazz Band. Buddy Tate was his replacement. This was the only time I heard a jazz band play for dancing in New York, and my first meeting with Red Richards, Herb Hall, and Buddy Tate, who must have talked to me nonstop during one of their thirty-minute breaks. Many years later Herbie and Red became my good friends when we recorded and went on the road together in my own band, the Original Camellia.

A TALE OF HERB HALL

One of the most influential musicians in my life was the clarinetist Herb Hall. We were together on several tours with Bob Greene's World of Jelly Roll Morton between 1978 and 1980. Because of him, I discovered I had been playing several tunes incorrectly. Herbie showed me the right notes and subtle differences between what I had been playing and what was correct, even to the extent of suggesting a more swinging timing of the melodies.

"How do you do that?" I would ask. "How do you swing that tune?"

"Oh, you'll get it one day," he'd say.

A distinguished-looking gentleman, his dress sense was as sharp as his playing. He played the modified Albert system one-piece clarinet that he had inherited from his brother Edmond Hall. I was immediately impressed with Herbie's memory for the correct melody and harmonies on a seemingly endless number of songs, and his ability to continuously create fresh variations. His playing was an elegant balance of sophisticated technique and simplicity. His sound was unmistakably New Orleans.

Herb Hall was born in 1907 in Reserve, Louisiana, a small town on the Mississippi River about forty-five miles above New Orleans by the river road, the youngest of eight children. Herb's first instrument was the guitar.

Their father, Edward Hall, played the E-flat clarinet in a local band called the Onward Brass Band (not the same as the Onward in New Orleans). Never learning to read music, although a teacher came out from New Orleans at regular intervals to teach them, Edward memorized his parts. As brass bands were very popular at that time, the Onward was keen to learn all the latest pieces, and in 1886 they even played in a contest in New York City.

Herb was around music as far back as he can remember. He explains: "Kid Thomas lived about two hundred feet away. And between where he lived and I lived there was a dance hall. Bands used to come from New Orleans, Baton Rouge, and Donaldsonville. There were bands across the river. Kid Ory and Pops Foster were from across the river. A burial society called the Bienfaisance Society owned the hall and promoted the dances. The band would play a number or two on the levee before the dance so the people across the river would know where the dance was going on."

A self-taught musician, Herbie was playing tenor banjo with his godfather by 1923. The band line-up was violin, cornet, trombone, banjo, piano, bass, and drums. Herb began learning to read music after he bought an alto sax. However, he never took any music lessons.

Herb and Robert Hall, behind Preservation Hall, 1980.
Photo: Judy Cooper, courtesy of New Orleans Records.

Due to his interest in music, Herb did not stay in Reserve much longer. His brother Clarence, who had started out playing the six-string banjo with Kid Thomas, was living in Baton Rouge and playing sax with Kid Victor's Jazz Band. Around 1926 Clarence left for New Orleans, and Herbie went out to Baton Rouge to replace him. The band had a violin, two saxes, trumpet, trombone, piano, banjo, bass, and drums. Herb recalls: "Kid Victor's band was a professional band. They had more jobs and played more out-of-town bookings, but it was basically the same type of band as my godfather's. They played by ear, but Claiborne Williams had more polish; they used music. The bands were softer when they used violin and guitar. But none of the bands were too loud. They played popular tunes, blues and waltzes. 'Jazz' numbers were played occasionally but were not very popular. A dance would be from 8 p.m. to 4 a.m. After every set the band would pick up a march and the men would escort the ladies off the floor and treat them to some refreshments outside."

Herb moved to New Orleans in 1927, as he had a sister and two brothers there already. Both brothers Clarence and Robert Hall were playing with Papa Celestin's band.

Herbie soon joined Sidney Desvigne.[1] He played lead alto, but practiced on his clarinet. Herbie continued: "Besides popular tunes, the band would play stuff like Louis Armstrong records. As soon as Louis's latest record came out, everyone went down to the record store and listened to it. And everyone was imitating Louis and Kid Ory. Occasionally there would be a jam session if Fate Marable's band came through on one of the boats. Guy Kelly was one of the top trumpet players. He had a bigger sound than the other guys. Son Johnson was the up and coming sax player. Son was one of the few to have any advanced musical training at that time."

In 1929 Herbie met Don Albert, who had been in San Antonio with Troy Floyd's band. Don had returned to New Orleans and was playing with Bebe Ridgley's band in one of the hotels, which was most unusual for an African American band in those days. When Don Albert got a booking in Dallas, he took part of the men from Ridgley's band and part of the men from Sidney Desvigne's.[2] It was here that Herbie met his wife, Annie, and they were married in 1931. The band increased in size when they went on tour, adding Alvin Alcorn on trumpet.[3] They did well on the road because the people had heard them first on the air. They played dances all over the South, the Midwest, and the East Coast (mostly for African American audiences) and were paid a basic price plus a percentage of the gate. Herbie recalls:

It's a good thing we were young, because we didn't make much money and things were worse than tough. Traveling was hard because there were no black hotels except in the big cities. We'd hear about where we could stay by word of mouth.

We'd stay at a private house and eat with the family. It took a long time traveling from place to place since there weren't any paved highways; the roads were dirt and gravel. The bus had trouble climbing mountains like in Virginia and Kentucky. The engine would get hot and cut out, and the brakes wouldn't hold the bus from slipping backwards. So when that happened, we'd jump out of the bus and grab large rocks we had ready on the back of the bus and chock the wheels. We called ourselves the "Rock Squad!"

When Billy Douglass was added on trumpet, they convinced Don Albert to front the band and let Alvin Alcorn take over on lead trumpet. They recorded eight sides in San Antonio in 1936. "In those days a recording company would travel to a city with the equipment and set up for a couple of weeks, and then move on to some other town." On those records, Herb played lead alto and baritone solos, Louis Cottrell tenor sax and clarinet. When the band broke up in 1940, Herbie returned to his home in San Antonio.

As soon as the war ended, Herbie and Annie went straight to New York, where they arrived in November 1945. His brother Ed Hall took him to the musicians' union and, by pulling a few strings, got him membership in two weeks' time. Immediately, Herbie went out with Herman Autry's five-piece group playing tenor sax, until he landed a steady gig in 1948 with the trumpet player Harvey Davis at the Club Cinderella. He played alto and tenor sax for the floor shows, and clarinet for the dance sets. Staying there until 1955, Herbie then toured Europe and North Africa with Sammy Price for three months, and recording with Sidney Bechet.

On his return to New York, Herbie played Dixieland gigs. When his brother Edmond left Eddie Condon's in 1955 to join Louis Armstrong, Bob Wilbur took his place. When Bob left the band in 1958, Herbie took *his* place. Besides working at Condon's, Herbie made many trips out of town, touring with the likes of Bobby Hackett, Wild Bill Davison, Red Richards, and Don Ewell. A mutual admiration instantly grew up between Herbie and the latter. Herbie recalls how once they played a gig for three nights straight without repeating a single tune.

It is obvious that Herb Hall had paid his dues in the music business many times over since the days he played with his godfather's band in Reserve. But who were the musicians he learned from most? Did he have any favorites?

I never collected records or imitated anyone on records, but I like Jimmie Noone. I heard him in San Antonio during the war. He played two nights with his quartet. He died not long after that. I liked to hear Omer Simeon too. I heard him with Sidney de Paris. My wife buys the records. A lot of people say I sound like my brother, but it is purely coincidental. In fact, I never heard my brother play until I went to New York with Don Albert the second time in 1936 or '37. When you learn by ear, you learn to play the right things when the band is playing the right things. It is important to have a good piano player with you. I could always remember a melody after I heard it and played it, and you played a lot of melody on lead alto, so that helped. The New York musicians I worked with, especially the pianist Sonny White and the guys at Condon's, played right, so I learned to play the right melodies and harmonies on the song.

I don't listen to my own records much because then you start playing the same thing over and over. I hate repetition. Whenever I play, I like to play with fresh ideas. That's why I don't listen to myself. My advice to younger players is this: Don't listen to any one musician all the time, especially when you are a beginner. Listen to all the guys if you want to sound like yourself.

In 1962 Herbie was introduced to yoga, something that profoundly changed his lifestyle and playing as well: "I was born in the Catholic Church but all my life there was something missing. I didn't know what it was until I began to get into yoga, Eastern philosophies, and vegetarianism. Yoga has helped me mentally. It opens the mind and you can think freer. There are no blockages and the breathing exercises have helped keep my mind young at this late stage of life. Musically, it seems I have improved to the point that I have started a new life."[4]

A TALE OF TEDDY BUCKNER

At the Hello Louis concert, successive musical periods in Armstrong's life were represented by different bands, and it fell to Teddy Buckner to play "West End Blues," perhaps Armstrong's most celebrated recording. Buckner played this on a regular basis, for he made no secret of the fact that Armstrong was his greatest idol. But that turned out to be his problem. The day before the concert I was lucky enough to meet him for the first time, and he was as friendly and open about himself as all the New Orleans musicians had been when I first encountered them. But there was no doubt he was extremely nervous about playing Armstrong's most celebrated piece right in front of him. Whether from nerves or not, Buckner had developed a big fever blister in the middle of his lip, which made it difficult and quite painful to play. The moment came and the opening cadenza was, indeed, a disaster!

Nevertheless, I felt the audience seemed to understand Buckner's predicament and panic attack. He redeemed himself somewhat by demonstrating at the end of the tune, as he slowly walked past the mic to the front of the stage, that his tone was so big and fat he could fill the auditorium with his sound without amplification.

Jazz critic Leonard Feather's review of the concert appeared a couple of days later in the *Los Angeles Times* and, despite Floyd Levin's plea to omit any reference to Buckner's embarrassing moment, he reported it factually as it happened. I wished, at least, Feather had shown some empathy for the position in which Buckner found himself, with some reference to being human.

Was that the end of the story? Not quite. I happened to be passing through Los Angeles a couple of years later, and coincidentally, Floyd and Lucille Levin were giving a jazz party and were gracious enough to extend an invitation to me as well. The many wonderful musicians present, who included Barney Bigard, Joe Darensbourg, Maxim Saury, Mike DeLay and Teddy Buckner, all took turns providing the music. As the sun was setting, Buckner turned to Feather, who was at the piano, and said:

"Let's play 'West End Blues.'"

"OK," said Feather, as he experimented with the piano break.

As you can imagine, Buckner played with a big, fat, warm tone, and his rendition was relaxed, confident, and sublime. All was well until the piano finale. Feather fumbled it badly, and Buckner picked up the ending beautifully so as not to draw attention to the inept piano break. Sitting right next to him at the time, I think I was the only one to notice the irony of the moment. Nobody said anything, but I remember a big wide grin on Teddy Buckner's face.

CHANGING TIMES

A new club, the Maison Bourbon, had opened on Bourbon Street, followed in the next few years by many others. In a new era of steady work for musicians, black and white, it was not long before I found myself employed part-time on "the street" as well. The black and white locals of the musicians' union had merged, and wages were becoming standardized. The increasing pay scale for parades began to put a strain on the finances of the African American "social aid and pleasure" clubs that hired the brass bands, and over the next few years non-union brass bands gradually took over the work from the established union bands that were expecting to get paid more.

Seeing the Young Tuxedo, my old band, play a parade shortly after my return, and all the old faces, made me feel quite at home again.

"Hey, man, *you* should be playing!" said the trumpeter Teddy Riley. "This is *your* gig."

"No, no, Teddy. I've been away two years. It's your gig now."

But as it happened, Thomas Jefferson dropped out, as he was playing six nights a week at the Paddock Lounge on Bourbon Street, Teddy stayed on as first trumpet, and Andrew Morgan hired me back.

Shortly after that, a group of us jazz fans went to see a weekend parade with Doc Paulin's Brass Band, the most popular non-union band around. We had been going to parades for years, but the atmosphere seemed tense that day. Something was wrong, but

I wasn't paying attention to the change of mood. I wasn't expecting trouble. All of a sudden as the band turned a corner, I found myself surrounded by angry young blacks. Bang! I was hit on the side of the mouth.

"Oh shit! You've got the wrong guy." I was in shock.

"Leave him alone, he ain't done nothin," said the girls who were also in the crowd. Miraculously, they backed off and let me go. I caught the bus back to Pat Brothers's place on Royal Street where I was staying temporarily, nursing my split lip. Later I found out from the others that they too had been chased by an angry mob. But an older black man rescued them, yelling "jump in" as he drove up. The kids were beating on the side of the car as he drove off.

Later I heard that, the day before, some white cops had beaten up a group of black kids while they were in custody. Everyone was mad as hell about it and took it out on the first white guys they saw.

"Are you angry?" asked Pat.

"No." I said. "I'm hurt, I guess, but not angry. I just didn't expect it."

"Amazing," said Pat as she put an ice-pack on the side of my mouth.

"You know what happened to me," said Wardell, who was also living there. A gentle, quiet African American, Wardell worked nights as a security guard. I shook my head.

"I'll tell you," he continued. "A few years ago I was walking home at night when some white college kids spotted me as they drove by. 'There's one!' they yelled. 'Get him.' I ran around a corner as they jumped outta the car, but they jumped back in and drove around the block looking for me. I had to crawl under a house and wait until they gave up. I stayed there a couple of hours, lying in the dirt. I'd have been dead otherwise."

I was lucky to be hit on the side of the mouth, although I couldn't play the trumpet for a month. The split skin gradually healed, but my lip felt weak until the scar tissue finally dissolved about six months later.

At this time, I and others like Paul Crawford, who was a regular trombonist with the Olympia Brass Band, were excluded from certain parades that were held by new groups such as "Tambourine and Fan," as they wanted to raise the political and social awareness of African Americans and to help the kids get motivated and out of trouble. Black Pride was the watchword, and naturally they wanted everyone involved in their parade to be African American. After years of being treated as second-class citizens, it was the time to publicly assert their presence in the community and their pride in themselves. But this, too, indicated the change in the air.

My goal was to continue what I'd begun in Britain: continue with my trumpet lessons, play in rehearsal bands at either Delgado or Loyola University to improve my reading ability, and study music theory. Between all that and listening to the musicians at Preservation and Dixieland Halls, my life was full. I was back in the French Quarter, living an idyllic bohemian life.

The swingingest band in town was Louis Cottrell's, and I enjoyed sitting in with them at Dixieland Hall on Bourbon Street. "You're an entirely different trumpet player now," said Cottrell. When his trumpet player Alvin Alcorn left for a tour in Britain and Europe, Cottrell hired me to play in his place for three of their gigs. It was a great honor.

The Maison Bourbon decided to try out a daytime band on the weekends and asked me to bring in a quartet. I had Harry Shields, brother of the Original Dixieland Jazz Band's Larry Shields, on clarinet, "Little Dad" Moliere on piano, and Alvin Woods on drums. Shields died right after that, so I got Albert Burbank to play clarinet. We were laid off soon after, but that spring, Your Father's Mustache asked me to bring in a quartet to play on Sunday afternoons. Alvin Alcorn had played the gig the summer before, but he was now working at Commander's Palace for the Sunday Brunch,[1] so he recommended me. I realize now that it was normal in New Orleans for a musician to recommend one of his students as a replacement. I hired Burbank, Little Daddy, and Alex Bigard on drums. This became a popular hangout for many of the fans and musicians who liked to sit in—men like Kid Thomas. The problem was Bigard was going very deaf and played out of time with the band on many tunes.

"Look, he's deaf. Either he goes or I go," said Burbank to me at the end of one Sunday. That was a terrible moment. Should I have quit the job? I don't know. It was a moment I wish had never happened. In the event I called up Bigard and let him go. He was angry and refused to understand, but I hired Cie Frazier, and later Al Babin, to play in his place. As our summer gig came to an end, the managers from the Maison Bourbon came in and hired me back for the afternoon slot at the weekends. In the end I got hired and fired at the club so many times I got used to it. It was a hard job, playing six hours with no air conditioning, but I needed the experience. This time I decided to call up the best available—why not? I got pianist Don Ewell, clarinetist Paul Barnes, and drummer Freddie Kohlman. When Ewell and Kohlman went on the road with Frank Assunto's Dukes of Dixieland, I replaced them with two of the Preservation Hall regulars, pianist Sing Miller and drummer Cie Frazier. Extraordinary though that may seem from today's vantage point, there wasn't much work in New Orleans for these men, and they were happy to take the two extra days a week for the short time it lasted.

When the Dukes' steady gig at Al Hirt's club folded, Freddie Kohlman took over the night spot at the Maison Bourbon, hiring Assunto on the trumpet. I was laid off again, but as it turned out, Freddie called me quite often to play whenever Assunto was taken ill. He was suffering from alcoholism and died a year or so later.

Unexpectedly, a quite different musical experience came my way when Raymond Ancar asked me to join his big band that played for carnival balls in the African American community. We used to rehearse at the musicians' union hall once a week, and played at least a dozen gigs during the season between Christmas and Mardi Gras. Conforming to the minimum union requirement in these larger venues such as the ILA Hall or the Autocrat Club, it was a ten-piece band with two singers. Traditional jazz was not normally played; rather, we would start with Count Basie and Ray Charles numbers and, as the evening progressed, draw more and more from the repertoire of Sam Cooke, Aretha Franklin, and other soul hits. I was lucky to play third trumpet in the orchestra for three seasons in the early 1970s. Several of our performers were well worth hearing on the odd occasion when they were featured. Wallace Davenport played first trumpet flawlessly and spent some time rehearsing the trumpet section. Julius Schexnayder (pronounced Shake-snyder) played baritone sax with the same rich tone as Harry Carney. Ed Frank played the piano and wrote out much of the Top 40 material. "Cookie" Gabriel and "Big Calvin" Spears were the featured vocalists. But Son Johnson on lead alto sax was *la crème de la crème*. I have never heard a more beautiful tone. He soloed as fluently and creatively as Charlie Parker, and played ballads like "Yesterday" with a sound like Johnny Hodges that would melt your heart. Other musicians told me that Son had studied advanced harmony and was playing what sounded like modern jazz by the early 1930s.

For me, opportunities to play music were infrequent, and became even less frequent when I enrolled in the music school at Loyola University. Studying music theory every morning and taking trumpet lessons in those days before telephone answering machines, I took few calls for gigs as I was hardly ever home. Although I was struggling to make ends meet, I was happy, learning much more about music, and feeling more and more at home living the life I chose in the French Quarter. On Dick Allen's recommendation I worked part-time in the afternoons in the rare books department at the Howard-Tilton Library at Tulane, with Seta Sancton, Tommy's mother, and under Bob Greenwood. It paid only minimum wage, but I began supplementing my income by playing music for tips on Royal Street and Jackson Square on the weekends with trombonist Scotty Hill. With the novelty of being the first band to do that, the tips turned out to be pretty good. It brought my income up to fifty-five dollars a week, which was exactly what I needed to live on in those days.

A TALE OF HAROLD DEJAN

Don't be sharp, be natural or you be flat!
—Harold Dejan

In a sense, Harold Dejan was the "King of the Streets." His Olympia Brass Band was the most hard-working band in town, playing the majority of the parades of the old-line Benevolent and Social Aid clubs. Percy Humphrey, leader of the much older Eureka Brass Band, was less and less interested in booking jobs ever since he'd been involved in a traffic accident in the 1960s and had difficulty walking. Yet Harold was always looking ahead to future prospects, as he sensed the changing times and the fresh opportunities that were developing. Always encouraging us 'jazz pilgrims' to sit in with the Olympia, Harold looked on us proudly as his musical children, occasionally putting some of us, like Tommy Sancton and myself, on the payroll. I played the Zulu Parade on Mardi Gras three years in a row. Now that jazz brass bands were becoming accepted by the whole community, and not just in the African American world, he was keen to appear in any and all events, both local and national.

"Play with me at the opening Saints game at Tulane Stadium," he said one day, speaking of the New Orleans football team. "Jaffe's hired the Eureka band, when he should have got *me*! But I'll show him! I have friends who want the Olympia." We went on at half-time, but following the Eureka. Many of Harold's men, who also played in the Eureka, chose to stay loyal to Harold as he gave them more work. We played louder than the Eureka, so I expect Harold felt he had won that battle. His goal was to win Jaffe over to book *him* instead of the Eureka, to make Jaffe his principal agent, and begin playing at Preservation Hall. As I found out, he would stop at nothing to achieve this.

"Hey! I've got the off-night at Crazy Shirley's. Can you play on Sunday?" It was David Paquette, Fred and Filly's piano playing son, when we met at Preservation Hall one night.

"Sure. Who's in the band?"

"I figure we've got to really knock 'em out, so I've got Harold Dejan on alto and Chester Jones on drums."

"Sounds good to me."

Crazy Shirley's was just three doors away from Preservation Hall on the corner of St. Peter and Bourbon. And we made some noise. Harold put the microphone in the bell of his alto sax and blew like hell all night.

"Watch me," he told me with that coy smile of his. "I'm 'onna go get the Sunday night at the Hall. We're going to do so good here that Jaffe's goin' to *have* to hire me."

A couple of Sundays later, I met the guys outside Preservation Hall only to find Kid Sheik and Chester Jones standing there looking glum. David Paquette came up to me:

"Look," he said, "Harold's taken over the band and hired Sheik on trumpet. Did he call you?"

"No, nobody told me anything!"

"That's not right!" Chester chimed in. "Look, Kid, that's how the 'pie-ass' is. He's supposed to give you a week's notice."

"But he's got Sheik," I said, with a kind of empty, hollow feeling inside. "I wouldn't mind if he'd called . . ."

Sheik jumped in: "It's your gig. You have to play this week and I'll start next Sunday. That's only right."

And so I did, then walked away from it. Dejan, who had been breaking me into the New Orleans scene perhaps more than any-one, had fired me without notice, and I was devastated. Much later, I realized I had become just another member of the pool of New

Orleans musicians, needed at times, but also a potential competitor for gigs. No longer getting special treatment as an apprentice, I had to stand on my own two feet from now on. It marked a big shift in my experience of playing music in the city.

Two or three weeks later, Jaffe hired Dejan and his band to play the Sunday nights at Preservation Hall. Dejan, in turn, hired Jaffe to play the bass horn in his band, and the partnership between them was to last many years.

Inexplicably, a few years later I got another call from Dejan to play second trumpet in the Olympia Brass Band on their first tour booked by Jaffe and Preservation Hall.[2] "Look," said Harold. "Sheik can't make it so they want you in the band."

Perhaps Jaffe had something to do with it. In any case, the money helped—I was studying music at Loyola and struggling to pay the bills.

LA DOLCE VITA

Better live while you can, be a long time you won't.
—Mabel Carter, Kid Sheik's sister

It was one of those gray, cool days in early November, a couple of months after my return to the city in 1970, when St. Louis Cathedral was holding its annual fair in Jackson Square. All the French Quarterites were there; Johnny Donnels, the photographer with his studio on the corner of St. Peter and Royal Streets; Bob Greenwood, the rare book specialist at Tulane University who had helped promote George Lewis's career in the early fifties; Gypsy Lou Webb of the Outsider Press; Dick Allen, curator of the Hogan Jazz Archive; Don Marquis, curator of the Jazz Museum; and Kid Thomas Valentine, the trumpet player and band leader from Algiers across the river.

"Hi Kid Thomas!" I was always a little unsure of how to address him.

"Hey! This is Barbara Reid. She's the lady who started Preservation Hall."

"That's right! You tell him!" said Barbara, glaring from behind her thick glasses.

I looked over at her. Who was this slightly built little woman with bright red lipstick and black hair that contrasted so much with her extremely white complexion? And why was she hanging out with Kid Thomas?

"I'd heard it was Ken Mills," I said, "but it was *you*?"

"You tell him, Thomas." She was getting angry now.

Kid Thomas grinned, flashing his bright, white teeth. "No, *she's* the one. She started it and that's the truth!"

"Oh. Will you tell me all about it?"

"Maybe one day," she said grudgingly, then added, peering suspiciously over her glasses: "so you're the young white guy who's been playing in the parades."

Whoa! I thought. She definitely doesn't approve. Better be careful what I say. Although I'd heard rumors about her for some time, of her interest in Voodoo, and of being involved in Preservation Hall when it started in 1961, for some reason our paths had never crossed. These days Barbara was a recluse, only rarely making a public appearance.

Some days later, I knocked on her door.

"Not now!" she yelled, and slammed the door in my face. But I was persistent and quite fascinated by her eccentric behavior. On my third attempt she let me in. She lived with her ten-year-old daughter Kelley in a run-down apartment in the 500 block of St. Philip Street. The room we sat in was dark, but as my eyes adjusted I could make out a collection of old paintings, statues, stacks of papers, a beat-up old typewriter, and bookshelves covering most of the available walls. She must have had over a thousand books. Had I walked into a Jean Cocteau movie set? Kelley was hovering toward the back of the apartment in her bedroom area, pretending to do homework.

After a glass of wine, Barbara began talking about these various objects, each one holding a memory, a precious memory to her. After many subsequent visits, details of her life gradually emerged. Besides my wish to hear about Voodoo and its history in New Orleans, we soon discovered a common interest in many topics besides New Orleans jazz, including politics, the Kennedy assassination, films of the classic 1950s and 1960s period, and the New Orleans trumpeter Lee Collins, whom Barbara had known in Chicago. She was passionate about Lee, whose playing clearly touched her on a deep level and, with her first husband Bill Reid, recorded him on several occasions in the early Fifties.

"You won't find many women who are as deeply moved by the music as I am," she confided in me one day. "That's one reason I don't go around listening to it anymore. I feel so strongly about it, and then because of what happened . . . ," she paused, "it's just too painful."

"What happened?"

"We started Preservation Hall because I could see it would be a big success if things were done right. It had to be just the music; let the musicians play their music in their own way, no drinks, no alcohol; so families and children could come in and hear it. That's what's important. Children have to hear it. And that way we'd be giving the musicians back their dignity. Most of them had been out of work so long, it looked like the music was dying.

"But really," she looked off into space. "You know the musicians started it."

"How was that?" I asked.

"Don't you see, Larry [Borenstein] asked them to come over to his gallery and play for free—just pick up some tips in a kitty basket. The musicians played for *free*. That did it. That was how the Hall started.

"In any case, you couldn't just go ahead and open a club in the French Quarter in those days. All the joints on Bourbon Street were run by the local Mafia and no outsider could move in on their turf. So I went to visit Carlos Marcello, the boss, and I acted real cute, you know." Here she peered over her glasses with a subtle smile, giving me the "Lolita look."

When I told him my idea and what I wanted to do, I think he was amused. I seemed so off-the-wall and non-threatening that he said go ahead and told his boys to lay off.

Barbara Reid in Chicago with African drums. Photo: Bill Russell, ca. 1951. Barbara Reid collection, gifted by Kelley Edmiston to the Clive Wilson collection.

We had a kitty on the door to pay the musicians and we guaranteed them union scale. We had this group of us who put it together—the New Orleans Society for the Preservation of Traditional Jazz. Ken Mills was the manager, I was the idea person and promoter, and dear Bill [Edmiston, her husband] paid the shortfall each night to make up the union scale. Here—I'll show you the books.

My priority was in getting the musicians working again and in getting their music heard by the kids. I think Ken's main interest was in experimenting with different combinations of musicians and then recording them for his Icon label.

Barbara went on to explain that they had subleased the building from Larry Borenstein, who had subleased it for his art gallery from Edmond "Beansie" Fauria, who in turn had leased it from an old lady who lived out of town. Beansie was the main Mafia contact with the black community, well-known for running a numbers racket.[1]

"We opened when Larry was away on an extended trip to California. You know who named it?—Slow Drag [Pavageau]—he gave us the name. When Larry got back he was furious and went around tearing down all our publicity posters. He thought naming it Preservation Hall was demeaning. He must have suddenly realized that it might be a commercial success, and he hadn't thought of it himself. So he told me that if it became a success, he'd take it away from me. He'd take back the lease."

"How did he manage it?"

Larry wanted us to get rid of Ken Mills, dissolve the society, and put Allan Jaffe in as the new manager. We had to vote on it, but I could see the writing on the wall. Bill [Edmiston] and I walked out and gave our proxy votes to [Bill] Russell. The vote was split, but Russell voted with Larry. That broke my heart. I haven't spoken to him since.

But the main thing is: the musicians are working, and Allan and Sandra Jaffe kept it going. That's what I always think of. You know Louis Cottrell [president of Local 496, the black local of the American Federation of Musicians], what he said to me? He said: "Barbara—say the word and I'll close it down." But I couldn't do that, not if it gave them work.

She gazed off into space for a moment.

"You know that contractor that Fred Paquette works for. Well, he's Mafia. He came to me and said if I said the word, he'd blow the place up in the middle of the night. And that would be that. Same thing; I told him 'No! The musicians have to work.'"

Barbara was clearly disillusioned, and not just with Larry Borenstein. From what I've pieced together from various stories she told me, it seems she first met Bill Russell in Chicago and they actually worked on a few projects together, recording Lee Collins, for example. In sharing a passion for New Orleans jazz and the musicians, they became very close. She even took time off from her family to accompany him on the first tour that Russell promoted with the great gospel singer Mahalia Jackson. When Russell left Chicago for New Orleans, Barbara left her husband Bill Reid behind and moved with her two children as well. As far as I know, the relationship with Bill Russell never went beyond that. But in making that decision to follow what her heart told her she must do, she nevertheless carried with her the grief of losing custody and all visiting rights with her children in the divorce that followed. She learned to live with her decision and buried her feelings by immersing herself in the life and abundant distractions of the bohemian French Quarter of the 1950s.

She was able to continue writing—she had taken journalism at the University of Chicago—with further lessons from Robert Tallant who taught at Tulane College. (Tallant had himself studied with Lyle Saxon, had contributed to *Gumbo Ya Ya*, and had written *Voodoo in New Orleans* and many other books.) And above all, finding it easy to become friends with the musicians, she went out to listen to them at the few surviving dance halls around the city where they still played at weekends. She wrote several evocative pieces about this for *Climax* magazine, one article beginning: "There was a time in the childhood of jazz when the Lake Pontchartrain shore was speckled with dance halls built out over the water . . ."

Not long after meeting Barbara, I asked her to tell me about Jim Garrison's investigation of President Kennedy's assassination.

"So why are *you* interested in the Kennedy assassination?"

"You know," I said, "I remember exactly where I was and what time of day it was when I heard the news. I was a student at

Newcastle University and I used to play around with long-range
radio and tune into Voice of America. They had a jazz program
by Willis Conover I liked. Well it was about five in the afternoon
and already dark outside. When they announced he'd been shot, I
was stunned. I told my roommate and he didn't believe me. When
Oswald was shot a couple of days later the first words out of my
father's mouth were: 'They did it.' You know, he meant the American intelligence community. So you see, I've always felt there was
enough suspicion to justify looking into it."

Barbara began to tell me of her work with Garrison's investigation of a possible conspiracy involving certain people who lived in
New Orleans.

> Kennedy was not popular with the majority of whites in this town.
> I was in the Bourbon House when it came on the news that he'd
> been shot. They cheered. It was chilling. And you know what?
> Nobody seemed surprised!
>
> You see those file cabinets over there? Those are Garrison's
> files on the case. He had me keep them here in case they disap-
> peared. And those over there [pointing into the dim interior of
> her apartment]—those are all the files that involved the Mafia.
> They were strictly off-limits. We ignored everything that con-
> cerned the Mafia. That was what you did, what you had to do.
>
> *They* led us on a wild goose chase.

I took her to mean whoever it was she felt was covering up the
truth. "They'd plant false leads all over town, phony signatures of
Oswald, all kinds of stuff. And my job was to run around and check
on them. Most of them turned out to be fakes, but we didn't know
it at the time."

There are many reasons why Garrison's investigation of Clay
Shaw collapsed. But for Barbara, it was yet another disillusionment.

The phone rang. I waited patiently while Barbara talked.

"That was a writer in Hollywood," she announced. "He's not the only one who calls."

"What about?"

"I give them ideas for television scripts."

I found this hard to believe until some years later when I met a writer from Los Angeles in Barbara's apartment. They had been sitting together all day, and this guy was busy taking down everything she said for his next project.

"You know *Hill Street Blues*, the cop TV series set in Chicago?" said Barbara. "That was my idea. It's a big hit, but I never get the credit."

"Oh?" I said. "Nice play on words."

Another time, when Woody Allen was in town recording the Preservation Hall Jazz Band for his movie *Sleeper*, we played together at a jam session. Afterwards I told him:

"There's somebody I want you to meet. Can you come?"

"Sure, let's go," he replied, asking no questions.

We walked over to Barbara's apartment, and when she opened the door, she could hardly believe her eyes. They embraced, and didn't stop talking for two hours. They had so many friends in common going all the way back to the Second City Players in Chicago. I have rarely seen Barbara so happy. Naturally she had several ideas for his next movies, particularly one that would involve undercover activities in New Orleans.

"Don't tell me," warned Woody. "I never, *ever*, use anyone else's ideas."

I began to realize that Barbara had a gift for seeing future trends, and for having the vision that an idea like Preservation Hall could succeed, though somebody else would always have to follow it through. I remember when the price of bread went up from thirty to forty cents a loaf. "You'll see," she said. "It'll be a dollar a loaf by next year." Her intuition proved to be right—double-digit inflation was right around the corner.

"What this town needs," she said one day, "is another jazz hall with food and drinks, trestle tables, checkered table cloths, a low bandstand with an old-fashioned wooden railing around it and a dance floor."

I could see it in my mind's eye, because she was describing what Lenny's On the Turnpike was like in Massachusetts, where I had once heard Count Basie.

"We could do it," she said, "with the right money. It will have to be in a converted warehouse on Decatur Street."

This was quite a stretch of the imagination, as Decatur Street in those days was completely dead at night. No tourist in his right mind would venture into this lower end of the French Quarter; there were only longshoremen's bars and restaurants that were open for breakfast and lunch. That was it. One night we took a walk around the old Farmers' Market and the warehouses, Barbara pointing out a couple of possible locations.

"People really want this kind of thing," she explained. "They like informality, and they'd love listening and dancing to a real New Orleans jazz band. Don't you see? We'd have busloads of people with the right promotion."

Even the streetlights seemed kind of dim in this abandoned end of town, and we did not notice a man in overalls walking toward us.

"What are you two doing?" he asked.

"Oh, just looking around, that's all," replied Barbara. He shrugged and walked off. But two minutes later a couple of police cars drew up next to us. He'd evidently called them to check us out. It was weird, but not unexpected by Barbara.

"Need some help? You lost or something?"

"No, no. We live near here."

"Better get on home then."

But once again, Barbara's intuition proved correct. Within a few years the Flea Market opened at the bottom end of the Farmers' Market and began to draw people, at least in the daytime. Storyville, a new music club, opened in one of the locations Barbara had pointed out on Decatur Street, but unfortunately it was badly managed and closed down after two or three years. It is now Margaritaville. A few years later, George Buck moved his record company to New Orleans, converting another old warehouse on Decatur Street, and Nina Buck opened the Palm Court Jazz Café underneath.

Barbara took it upon herself to expand my education, introducing me to many ideas and writers that were new to me. Her recommended top five list of books were *Psychology and Alchemy* by Carl Jung; *Five Plays* (which included *Orphée*) by Jean Cocteau; *The Joker* by Jean Malaquais; *Dahomey: An Ancient West African Kingdom* by Melville Herskovits; and *The Wandering Jew* by Eugene Sue, all of which I read with great interest except Sue, which was altogether too turgid, even for me.

Coincidentally, I saw Cocteau's *Beauty and the Beast* right after finishing *Psychology and Alchemy* and recognized it as an alchemical drama—a journey of self-realization, culminating with the "mystical union of opposites" that Jung wrote about.

"What was it like, seeing it?" she asked.

I paused. "A religious experience."

"That's my boy," she laughed.

Fellini's film *La Dolce Vita* was another that we talked about. Barbara resonated strongly with its central theme—disillusionment. "Did you notice what happened to the lead character?" she asked. "One by one, all his ideals and beliefs in his heroes were crushed. At the end he was left with *nothing* to believe in; he was devastated. The sweet life was empty." Years later I realized she was telling me, obliquely, her own story.

Dahomey gave me a complete picture of West African religion and the way it permeated every aspect of that civilization, and hence the background to the survival of that religion and African cultural traits in the New World.

"Did you notice," she said once, "the gods come when they are called by the drums? Each god has his or her own rhythm. The drums are sacred, you see, and to become a drummer you have to spend many years as an apprentice." I began to realize that music, especially the music that moved us, held this implicit, sacred element that had somehow survived the transition from Africa.

Barbara continued, "Baby knew this"—Warren "Baby" Dodds, brother of clarinetist Johnny Dodds, was one of the greatest drummers to come out of New Orleans—"and he treated his drums with reverence. I asked him once how he kept his drum heads so clean?

"'They're skins,' he replied. 'How do you wash your face? I do the same with my skins. I wash them with soap and water.'"

Barbara's interest in Voodoo, beginning as part of an anthropology study in Chicago, continued in New Orleans. She immersed herself in it, learning firsthand from several of the local priestesses and "doctors" including Reverend James and Miss Pearlie. Once she made a *gris-gris* to cast a spell on the developer of the Bourbon Orleans Hotel, because the Black Carmelite nuns who had a convent there were pressured to sell out and resettle elsewhere.

"I don't really believe in it," she confided. "I think the human mind has the capacity to project and interpret things in any way it wants. And that's how divination readings seem to work. But," she continued about the developer, "the strange thing is: within a year, that man lost his entire financial empire and went bust."

"That's amazing. Tell you what—do you read cowry shells like in Africa?"

"I've got them right here," she said, pulling out a white bag. She threw them across the rug on the floor, took one look at the pattern they made and took in a sharp breath.

"I'm not doing it," she said and put the shells back in their bag.

"What was it?" I wanted to know.

"Never you mind," she said sharply.

"What about cards? Will you read mine?"

"Oh!" she smiled. "I can, but I don't usually do that anymore. I got out of Voodoo when it started to feel dangerous. But OK, let's see, I won't do a full reading. Look here," she continued, turning over the cards. "They say you will be a writer someday."

"No way! I'm not a writer. I play the trumpet."

"They say you will be. The cards never lie—only people do. Let's see your palm. Well here it is again. You have two lines there which means you have two areas of creativity."

"What do the cards say for you?" I asked. Barbara became defensive and changed the subject in a hurry. But something of her fears emerged later. One day I asked her if I could drive her across Lake Pontchartrain to visit old friends of hers who used to live in the French Quarter.

"No, I could never go," she announced. "I'm afraid of water."

"Why, for heaven's sake?"

"Now, don't laugh. The cards said I would die of drowning."

"But Barbara, you don't believe that, surely. You know you can die of drowning if your lungs fill up with fluid."

"I know *that!*" She was really angry and kicked me out.

I continued to visit Barbara about once a week, finding our conversations extremely stimulating. There was always a bottle of wine open. One evening she announced she was famished and, since her daughter Kelley was sleeping over with the neighbors across the street, could we go to dinner at Ruffino's in the next block? A long-established traditional Italian restaurant on St. Philip Street, it was fairly empty that night. We ordered, and as we began eating our main course, Barbara leaned over to me and groaned.

"Oh, no," she whispered. "See that table at the back?" I looked and there was a long head table on a raised platform with about a dozen men in suits having dinner.

"What of it?" I asked.

"I know who they are," she whispered. "They're all Mafia, and this must be a formal business dinner. Who knows?"

And that could have been that, as far as I was concerned. But when they left, each one of them came over and paid his respects to

Barbara, bowing to her in all seriousness. She acknowledged them all individually, but was absolutely mortified. There she was having dinner with a twenty-nine-year-old. It looked like we were having an affair, though nothing could have been further from the truth.

Barbara was frequently on the phone with countless friends from all over the States, discussing the news, politics, the latest movie, or perhaps a conspiracy theory. Ever since she began working for the Garrison investigation of the Kennedy assassination she had always assumed her phone was bugged, but lived her life openly and unafraid. One night we had been discussing the curious case of the son of J. M. Kaplan, a man with strong CIA connections, who was incarcerated in a Mexican jail. The story had been written up in *Ramparts* magazine. It seemed that father and son had fallen out and it suited the father, or the CIA, to leave him in jail. When I called Barbara the next day, her phone was dead. After a few days trying to reach her by phone, I walked over to see her. When I knocked on the door, she quickly opened it and dragged me inside.

"Did you hear what happened?" she exclaimed. "They've busted Kaplan's son out of jail, and cut off my phone."

"Why would they do that?" I asked.

"Don't you see? We were talking about it the night before, as if we knew what was going to happen. Normally with something like this, people call me from all over to find out more or tell me what's going on. Anyway, the telephone company says they're looking into it. Can't promise when they'll fix it."

A later report in *Ramparts* stated that the CIA had bribed the guards, sent a helicopter into the middle compound of the jail, and lifted Kaplan's son out in broad daylight. The armed guards had simply turned their backs.

It was *three weeks* later before the repairmen, all five of them in overalls, came over to check on Barbara's telephone line. They took several hours taking the phones apart and putting them back together again. It was all very unusual. Were they installing new, updated bugs? Barbara certainly thought so.

I sometimes brought friends, usually jazz fans from overseas, to see Barbara, who gradually became comfortable with meeting people again. When the English drummer Trevor Richards came back to visit New Orleans, he also enjoyed these long nights at Barbara's, talking over the music scene in Chicago, or the early days of Preservation Hall. He brought with him a recipe for a drink called a Nikolaschka: "The favorite drink of Nikolas, the last Czar of Russia," he announced.

Barbara beamed. "Now *that* I'd like to try." She warmed to Trevor immediately.

"You take a shot glass of vodka (originally cognac) and place a slice of lemon across the top," he began. After we had prepared three such glasses he continued:

"Now make a small pile of very finely ground coffee on top of the lemon, and some sugar on top of that." I fetched a mortar and pestle from the kitchen and began grinding.

"Then you do this." Trevor picked up the lemon with all the ingredients and bit it off at the rind. Chewing it up without swallowing for as long as he could, he then emptied the vodka into his mouth in one go and continued swilling the mixture around for a moment before swallowing.

"Aahh!" [Try this at home.]

When it was my turn a small explosion went off in my head, but I felt strangely elated. It was a wake-up rush. That first night on nikolaschkas lasted until daybreak—we drank a round about every half hour—yet I was wide awake and felt quite sober. We went over to the Café du Monde in the French Market and watched the sun rise over the West Bank of the river, which is one of the delightful anomalies of New Orleans. The Mississippi curves around so much, the sun rises over the West Bank when viewed from the French Quarter and most of Uptown.

I think it was Trevor who suggested that Barbara throw a jam session party like the ones we used to go to in the sixties. And so Barbara finally came out of reclusion and opened up her house. All the resident foreign musicians were there of course, along with local musicians like Kid Sheik, Louis Nelson, Kid Thomas, Danny Barker, Manny Sayles, and Father Al Lewis. As the music wound down in the early hours of the morning, clarinetist Jacques Gauthe, who was the chef at the Plimsoll Club, bought several dozen eggs at the twenty-four-hour grocery in the French Market and started cooking omelets, throwing the empty eggshells over his shoulder at the wall behind. An ecstatic moment!

Barbara was so happy. It was like a return to her good old days of the French Quarter in the fifties, but with different faces. I overheard a comment from one of the guests: "It's interesting. Clive plays a bit like everyone." To which Barbara responded: "Yes, but I like it best when he comes up with his own ideas."

In spite of Barbara's increasing disillusionment, there was always one element in her life which lifted her spirits and that was the music, music when played with passion. The musician who spoke to her heart most directly was the trumpeter Lee Collins, whom she had known in Chicago. For Barbara, Lee's playing expressed the longing and the struggle of humanity for something higher, beautiful, free. It gave her hope. On occasion, she began visiting Preservation Hall again to sit with the tourists on the cushions against the wall near the band, loving every minute of it, chatting with Bill Russell as old friends, and even dancing one time with Allan Jaffe in the carriageway. It was reconciliation. The vision that Preservation Hall would succeed was hers: that it would succeed not only commercially but also give the musicians the dignity and recognition they deserved, provide a forum for millions of people from all walks of life and around the world to hear them in person. Under Allan and Sandra Jaffe's subsequent management, her dream became a reality.

Nevertheless, she was drinking too much and her health was steadily deteriorating, though none of us was sufficiently aware of these warning signs. She surprised me one day when she telephoned: "I want to go visit Bob and Effie across the lake. Haven't seen them in a long time. Can we all fit in your car?"

It was only a forty-minute drive to old Mandeville on the North Shore across the twenty-four-mile causeway, but once there, in their twenty-acre estate, Barbara relaxed. "Sanctuary!" she exclaimed, as we drove through the gates.

With hundreds of pine trees, live oaks, and exotic shrubs collected from around the world, with goats, two horses, a few cows, chickens, guinea fowl, and peacocks, Bob and Effie had created the nearest thing to heaven on earth, so peaceful and quiet. All stress seemed to melt away the minute you entered through the gates. After lunch Barbara got up and, walking with a cane these days, said she wanted to go out alone and look around. She sat in her favorite spot—the branch of a particular tree. About an hour later she came back and said: "Everything's OK. We can go home now if you like."

A week later, very early in the morning, I received a phone call from her husband Bill Edmiston: "There's been a tragedy," he began. "I came home from work and when I went to check on Barbara, there she was, sitting on the couch. But she's gone. She passed away in her sleep. We don't know any more yet."

Some days later, Bill told me the coroner's report. Barbara had walking pneumonia and her lungs had filled up with fluid.

A NATURAL LIVING

─────── ❧ ───────

People have to do an awful lot of funny things if they don't play music.
—Musician interviewed at the Hogan Jazz Archive, Tulane University

Though I was not making a living entirely by playing music, I was putting in more hours per week on the trumpet than ever before. New Orleans in the early 1970s offered myriad opportunities to continue developing as a musician. Besides rehearsing each week with the Raymond Ancar band, I was sitting in with the Loyola University stage band twice a week, where I also took music theory and trumpet lessons. I played an occasional parade, usually with the Young Tuxedo Brass Band, played weekends with Scotty Hill on Jackson Square, and sometimes substituted for another trumpet player in a Bourbon Street club as well. How did I get work? Living in the French Quarter and later the Faubourg Marigny nearby, listening to the musicians at Preservation Hall whenever possible, I was highly visible. Always finding at the end of the week that somehow I had made just enough to cover my living expenses, I became used to the condition of not relying on a steady job. My life was full, musically challenging, carefree, and happy.

Another activity that began to take up considerable time was New Orleans Records, the record company I had started with my friend Paige Van Vorst.

"His Master's Voice." Raymond Burke at home, 1972.
Photo: Justin Winston, courtesy of New Orleans Records.

Within a few months of issuing the *Kid Thomas at Kolhman's Tavern* LP, the clarinetist Raymond Burke asked me to put out the session he had made back in 1949 with "Wooden Joe" Nicholas, Johnny St. Cyr, and Joe Avery. This was a major surprise and a real scoop for us. Although four sides of *Ray Burke's Speakeasy Boys*, as it was dubbed, had appeared on Paradox 78s, the remainder of the session—coincidentally recorded in the back room of the New Orleans Record Shop—had supposedly disappeared. As it turned out, Raymond had been keeping it all along. Luckily it was on paper tape which, although it was brittle and required multiple splicing repairs, had not developed "print-through" or otherwise deteriorated. The quality of sound was the same as on the day Herbert Otto had recorded it. Raymond had welcomed the chance to play with these African American musicians, and the recording captured some of his most creative moments. We had a slight panic

Clive Wilson on Canal Street, 1973. Photo: Justin Winston, used by permission.

when the production company in Nashville, deep in the heart of the "Bible Belt," returned the tape with a note explaining they did not press pornographic records! The tune titled "All the Whores Like the Way I Ride" was causing the problem. Before they would agree to handle it, I had to explain this was an old traditional jazz tune and that, in any case, the track in question had no vocal.

Our next project, featuring the great New Orleans trumpet player Lee Collins—*A Night at the Victory Club*—essentially came from Barbara Reid. Lee has always been one of my favorites, and I loved to hear stories from Barbara's earlier days in Chicago of listening to Lee at the Victory Club and on occasion recording him with the help of Bill Russell. Barbara encouraged me to issue the best of those recordings. Unfortunately, I was able to pick out only five good tracks and needed more to make up both sides of an LP. Here Barbara Reid came to the rescue. I mentioned I had seen some acetates of Lee Collins with Don Ewell over at Joe Mares's shop, also recorded in Chicago in 1951.

"Those are mine!" Barbara exclaimed angrily. "You go back to Joe and tell him I said I want you to issue them!"

Joe meekly handed them over. Although a great admirer of Collins—he was the A&R man for the recording back in 1929 of the Jones and Collins Astoria Hot Eight—Joe didn't care to issue this particular session. By a happy coincidence the record came out at the same time as the publication of *Oh, Didn't He Ramble: The Life Story of Lee Collins as Told to Mary Collins*, ed. Frank J. Gillis and John W. Miner (University of Illinois Press). Capturing his emotionally charged and expressive playing, these informally recorded sides show Lee Collins's debt to both Bunk Johnson and Louis Armstrong.

A TALE OF BILL RUSSELL

Bill Russell was directly involved with the Lee Collins recording, for he had not only recorded Lee in the Victory Club for Barbara and Bill Reid, but also paid for all the expenses incurred at the time. Although Bill would never issue the Victory Club session himself—it included a tenor saxophone—he admired the intensity of Lee Collins's blues playing and his affinity to Bunk Johnson's trumpet style. He sold me the sides at cost. Originally I thought Bill was being obsessive about the money for, amazingly, he had kept the receipts for over twenty years—everything connected with the recording including the rolls of film he used to take photographs! It was all in a box labeled "Lee Collins." If I was to issue this recording, he insisted I pay him the exact amount, no more, no less. Then he proceeded to give me a lecture on my foolishness. "You're doing this the wrong way," he began. "Records are made to make a profit—didn't you know that? It's a simple fact." While I was delighted to buy the session at such a reasonable price, Bill had shown me that he had not made one cent profit from the venture!

Bill Russell and Barbara Reid holding the Lee Collins album *A Night at
the Victory Club*. Preservation Hall, 1978. Photo: Paige Van Vorst of
New Orleans Records, used by permission.

Gradually I came to realize that Bill Russell was teaching me,
always, one way or another—in this case, to draw my attention to
the greed or profit motive that lies behind most activities. However,
Paige Van Vorst and I were lucky with our label—New Orleans Records—when Allan Jaffe of Preservation Hall decided to feature our
LP of Kid Thomas on his nights there. It sold so well that it paid for
all our subsequent issues.

Yet the profit motive was abhorrent to Russell; the groundbreaking
recordings he had made in the 1940s for his American Music label
(AM) were not commercial, but made to promote and document the
New Orleans jazz musicians he loved, such as Bunk Johnson, Wooden
Joe Nicholas, and George Lewis. He carefully selected for issue only
those takes that showed them in their best light. Hearing an internal

component in music, perhaps sacred, the element that normally has no name that comes through occasionally with a few musicians, Russell aimed to capture it on record.

Bill's constant companions were an extended family of mice—they had taken up residence in his old amplifier—and a talking parakeet named Pretty Boy. Whenever I came in, the bird would fly off around the room and perch at a safe distance on top of the shelves. "That parakeet's got more brains in his head than you have!" Bill would say. "If he made just one mistake he'd be dead. But you—how many mistakes do you make in your life? He knows he can't afford to make even one mistake. I'd call that intelligence, wouldn't you?"

I laughed, but if you knew Bill at all, you knew he regretted at least one affiliation in his life. He discovered after World War II that the company he worked for was peripherally involved with the effort to develop the atom bomb. Although he was unaware of this connection at the time, even the tiny fraction of his livelihood derived from this effort was unacceptable. Being a pacifist, he refused to have anything to do with the military/industrial complex and the companies and people involved, which included politicians. When someone once asked him why he didn't vote, he replied: "I don't like to encourage them!"

Bill was a teacher in everything he did or said, in the way he lived his whole life. He taught by example. Once he made up his mind about something, he never compromised. He never wanted to be a part of anything he considered dishonest or destructive. Whatever he did, whether writing, answering questions, or simply sweeping up at Preservation Hall, he was always teaching. But it was not the kind of teaching that people generally recognized.

To visit Russell, you would think that here was a pack rat, a collector who could throw nothing away. But on closer inspection, as you climbed through the many cardboard boxes that were everywhere, on shelves, on the floor, on chairs, you would find that every box was labeled. Each one referred to some aspect of his work and research.

I used to visit Russell quite often, and before he would talk about subjects I was interested in, like the musicians and the way they played, or his experiences in Chicago with Mahalia Jackson, he would make me listen to him talk about a hundred and one other things such as the foolishness of human beings, the superior intelligence of his parakeet, and much more. In all of this he tried to stimulate fresh thought, an independent way of looking at things, and an awareness that I knew very little about what I was doing. He looked like a wise old guru, or perhaps a monk, with his bald head ringed by white hair. Although many tended to put him on a pedestal, he was forever trying to put us off by acting as an eccentric and by making it difficult for us to get anything out of him. Although he made himself available to all who came to see him, some left in frustration. Those who stayed long enough to get past his initial harangue usually had their questions answered. I think it was his way of sorting out those who were genuinely there to learn from those who had preconceived opinions and attitudes. He told one such self-appointed "authority" on early jazz to look into its Mexican origins. Then he told me he had deliberately sent this gentleman off on a wild goose chase to keep him busy for a few years, and off his back.[1]

Once I asked him about buying some of his American Music 78s. Before selling me what he had at an absolute bargain, he smiled and replied with a priceless example of circular thinking. "I really don't like to sell records to people like you who are stupid enough to buy them!"

But I learned that he respected me, too. Once I found him with a friend from Rutgers University Jazz Studies, completely absorbed in avant garde jazz recordings. He invited me to join them for a while and explained some of it to me, and what to listen for. They spent the whole weekend, day and night, absorbed in it. Having written avant garde percussion music back in the early thirties, Russell understood it. He had employed similar devices in the 1930s that these jazz musicians were using in the 1970s.

Another time, Russell was going through many of his unissued takes from the American Music recordings that a Japanese company, Dan Records, wanted to release. He had shelved these takes because he felt they sounded uninspired or boring, or perhaps there were simply too many mistakes. But the man from Dan was pressuring him to release a lot more. On one of these recordings Bill turned to me:

"What do you think, Clive? It sounds like crap to me."

"Yes," I replied. "I'm afraid it does."

But he gave in and allowed Dan Records to issue it anyway. Another track that Dan Records issued was "High Society" by the George Lewis band, Louis "Kid Shots" Madison on trumpet. Russell commented: "I've always thought it never quite made it, there's nothing much happening."

In that case I disagreed: "No, it's wonderful to hear how Kid Shots plays it. It flows, it's different."

"You see this?" he asked me another time, showing me a 78 of Bunk Johnson playing "Down by the Riverside." "The original title is 'Ain't Gonna Study War No More,' but I thought no one would press it during the Second World War, so I changed the name.[2] You know," he continued, his voice rising slightly with excitement, "'When the Saints Go Marching In' was never popular, even though Louis Armstrong had recorded it. I asked Bunk to record it, and when he started playing it in New York at the Stuyvesant Casino, it really took off. He had to play it every night."

By the early 1970s, the number of jazz fans and musicians visiting and revisiting New Orleans had exploded. Mike Casimir organized group tours from Europe every spring, coinciding with the annual New Orleans Jazz and Heritage Festival. We held jam sessions on Sunday afternoons at Bonaparte's Retreat, a bar on Decatur Street, where visiting musicians could play alongside their New Orleans idols. I remember one remarkable moment of this regular event. I was playing "Careless Love" the way Kid Sheik had shown me how it was played by the legendary Chris Kelly back in the 1920s. When it came time for my muted trumpet solo, Kid Sheik conducted the band behind me to play a three-beat stop time as bands used to do for Kelly. The place was packed, but suddenly everyone stopped talking and you could have heard a pin drop. It was unexpected, eerie, spine chilling.

After returning to New Orleans from a summer trip to San Francisco in 1973, I was pulled aside by one of the managers of the Maison Bourbon on the corner of Bourbon and St. Peter Streets: "Look," he said. "Cag's been taken sick and is in the hospital, and Dave Williams is looking for a trumpet player to take his place. Go talk to him."

Sadly, trumpeter Ernie Cagnoletti suffered from diabetes and had to have a leg amputated. Although he eventually recovered enough to play again at Preservation Hall, his Bourbon Street days were over. Pianist Dave Williams—"The Fat Man," as he was known—hired me on the spot. The gig was hard, with just four of us in the band playing six hours a day, six days a week without air-conditioning. Though exhausting, the money from playing a steady job for the first time in my life eased my financial worries.

Equally at home with both rhythm 'n' blues and New Orleans jazz, Dave would sing many of his own compositions. After several months of developing our own arrangements of his tunes, I recorded the band for New Orleans Records at a club on North Rampart Street called Lu and Charlie's. I picked an environment that was similar to many of the clubs like the Caldonia or the Club Desire where Dave had worked in the 1940s and 1950s. We aimed at producing a more natural recording than a slick studio production. I also issued the catchy song "I Ate Up the Apple Tree" as a jukebox single and it sold moderately well for several Carnival seasons.

Promoting a single, however, proved to be a very time-consuming, costly, and largely unrewarding activity. Dave would drive me around to the local black radio stations and told me *I* had to go in and get it played. He said they wouldn't listen to him because he was black, but if a white man walked in, they'd listen. It was the strangest thing, but he was right. As a result, Dave managed to gain some local fame and became known as "The Apple Tree Man." The song is still played today, achieving recognition through recordings by the Dirty Dozen Brass Band, Kermit Ruffins, and Dr. John.

Dave Williams, 1974. Photo: Barry Kaiser,
courtesy of New Orleans Records.

A TALE OF DAVE WILLIAMS

When Dave Williams sang the "Way Back O' Town Blues," he was remembering those small communities, lying back from Tremé toward Lake Pontchartrain, back of Desire and St. Bernard, that were originally settled by people who came in from the country, people who worked the plantations. As Dave told me: "The people would have what they called 'Blue Mondays.' They'd have a party instead of going to work on a Monday. They had down-to-earth music, stomp-down music, plenty of blues. And they'd dance like that, slow and easy [here he demonstrated a slow, belly-rubbing grind]. That was back o' town! I'm talkin' about *way* back o' town, you can believe what I'm tellin' you!"

Born in 1920 on Touro Street below the French Quarter, he was already playing piano by the age of five. His first music teacher was his mother, who played organ and piano at the First Free Will Baptist Church at Touro and Claiborne.

By the time he was twelve, Dave was playing "nickel parties" with other aspiring young musicians. As Dave explained:

That was during depression times and prohibition was still going on. Everything was a penny to a nickel; you paid a nickel to come in; and anything from a penny to a nickel for home-made ice cream, pies, and things like that. It was supposed to be for the children, but grown-up people would buy alcohol and water undercover.

A fish fry was like the same thing, but more open. They'd hang a red kerosene light on the gate, so everybody knew that was a fish fry. The people would sell fish and potato salad, and if they knew you, they'd sell you alcohol and water. Now, if the people talked too loud, made too much noise, the lady givin' the party, she'd say: "Hush, hush, speak easy!"

Saturday night fish fry! That was the most particular night it was given. That was the big day.

In three more years Dave had been chosen to play in an adult group with two of his relatives, Paul Barnes and Lawrence Marrero, both second cousins. They played at the Cadillac Club on St. Claude Avenue at the Industrial Canal. Dave's cousins took good care to pick him up, bring him home, and turn his pay over to his mother.

Shortly afterward, Dave had his own group at the San Jacinto Club. He was a working musician until entering the armed services in 1941; however, his first formal musical training did not come until 1948 when he left the service and began to study on the G.I. Bill. At that time he was playing many of the legendary New Orleans nightspots: the Caldonia, the Hideaway, the Dew Drop Inn (with Joe Turner and Lloyd Price), the Pelican Club, and the Club Desire. Dave recalled: "The big acts, the show acts went to the Pelican, but for down-to-earth music, the folks from the Ninth Ward liked to stay in their own neighborhood and they went to the Club Desire. That Desire was a beautiful place with the most beautiful dance floor and people could sit in a gallery that went all around the room. It was a *nice* place."

After attending music school, Dave joined the Freddie Kohlman band at the Mardi Gras Lounge on Bourbon Street, the beginning of many years of playing almost every club on the street. Dave was writing songs for years. "I think of the words and music at the same time. They come to me in my sleep and wake me up. I just go to the piano. They're so beautiful sometimes I hates to get up." He used to forget some of his songs until he bought a tape recorder. And how did his wife feel about those early hour sessions? "I've got me a good wife: she never complains. She gets up too sometimes, and then we sit around the table and drink coffee."

PAPA FRENCH

One learns so much more by being on the inside looking out
than by being on the outside looking in.
—Berta Wood[1]

My telephone rang one Sunday afternoon in the spring of 1973. It
was Bob French, the drummer with Papa French's Original Tuxedo
Jazz Band:

"How soon can you get here and make the gig? We're in Jackson
Square. Our trumpet player hasn't shown up."

"Give me five minutes," I said, jumping at the chance to play a
whole job with this well-known group. Originally Papa Celestin's
band, which had been in continuous existence since 1911, they included Papa French on the banjo, his son Bob on the drums, Joseph
"Brother Cornbread" Thomas (clarinet), Homer Eugene (trombone),
Frank Fields (string bass), and none other than Jeanette Kimball (piano), who had joined Papa Celestin's band as long ago as 1926.

From listening to them many times over the years, initially with
Alvin Alcorn and subsequently Jack Willis in the trumpet chair, I
knew what they liked. Since Jack Willis's retirement after coming
down with Bell's palsy, they had used others who were not so familiar with the New Orleans style of playing, and evidently not so
reliable either. So I simply played the lead as best as I could, which
was in the style of my idol at the time, Alvin Alcorn.

A year later, as Papa French continued to have problems with his trumpet players, he asked me to join the band. What a surprise! But everyone seemed pleased. Homer Eugene and "Brother Cornbread" showed me what I was expected to play on various tunes, and so I continued the routines that had originated with either Alcorn or Willis. As a result, I stayed with the band for three years.

The first thing Papa did was to take me to the clothing store where he bought his uniforms—a red jacket and white tie. Additionally, we wore tuxedos on certain jobs, and in the summer, white tuxedos.

We played a lot of what I would call Mardi Gras gigs—"society" jobs for the old-line Mardi Gras krewes and their members. As I was integrating the band for the first time, quite a few of them were surprised, questioning how a young white boy could play with a long-established African American band. But by the second Carnival season they had adjusted to seeing me and apparently liked my playing enough to enjoy seeing me fit in musically with their favorite band. Many of them remembered when Papa Celestin himself played for their parties. One of these older men, Charlie Carriere, told me in private how he had hung out with Louis Armstrong when they were kids, and how they had gone swimming together in the New Basin canal on many occasions. Although that sounds unlikely, it so happened that Armstrong's "dad" worked for the Carriere family business, which was located on the New Basin canal. They knew each other because young Louis would take his dad's lunch sandwich to him every day.

Papa French also played many parties in hotels for conventions, a relatively new and fast-growing business in the city during the 1970s. In those days, the musicians' union had many protective rules in place, one being that ballrooms and halls where music was played had minimum requirements. In most hotel ballrooms, the band had to be eight pieces. In halls rented out for carnival balls like the Autocrat or the ILA Hall, the band had to be ten pieces.

Papa French's Original Tuxedo Jazz Band, 1975. Bob French, Jeanette Kimball, "Cornbread" Thomas, Albert "Papa" French, Clive Wilson, Homer Eugene, Frank Fields. Promotional photo used by permission of George French, son of Papa French.

This meant that Papa French frequently hired two trumpets, and for my first two years in the band the second trumpet was none other than Dave Bartholomew. Dave, who had produced so many of the rhythm 'n' blues recordings of the 1950s and 1960s, was glad to come out and play to keep his lip in shape. In any case he enjoyed playing traditional jazz, which he did with great authority. Knowing all the tunes, he could improvise a second harmony part to my lead instantly. His firm, confident, driving style inspired me to play with more drive myself to keep up with him. Imagine what it was like for me to play first trumpet to Dave Bartholomew. He was always gracious and encouraging, and we took turns playing the trumpet solos.

When Dave went on the road with Fats Domino for one last time, Papa began using a variety of second trumpet players who had in the meantime become available, such as John Brunious,

Dalton Rousseau, and, once he was able to play again, Jack Willis. While Bartholomew was the strongest, Willis was the most inventive, ceaselessly constructing beautiful arabesques around my lead.

Although a couple of these trumpet players angled for my job, Papa French kept me on; he must have liked what I was doing. Eventually, the time came when Papa began to feel his age and turned over much of the band leading to his son Bob. By this time, John Brunious's younger brother Wendell had begun playing second trumpet with us, and when he turned twenty-one, Bob laid me off and hired Wendell. Though initially I felt quite rejected and hurt, as I had become used to being a member of the band, in reality I knew it had to be, and that it was natural for my three-year tenure to come to an end.

Looking back, I realize that until this time almost all my work had come because the New Orleans musicians had hired me to play with them—a great honor and very much an unexpected result of my move to the city. But the time had come for me to branch out and take the initiative in my own career. Musicians used to call this "Every tub on its own bottom."

A TALE OF JACK WILLIS

My admiration for Jack Willis's cornet playing began one night in 1967 when he substituted in Kid Sheik's band at Preservation Hall. With "Sing" Miller at the piano and "Achie" Minor on the banjo, he cut his style back to the bare bones, but it was every bit as musical. Playing with a fine control throughout the night with few elaborations, his lead quietly took command, rising and falling with the swinging pulse of Chester Zardis at the bass and Chester Jones on the drums, and providing a foil for Capt. Handy's driving alto sax. As a feature I remember him playing, in complete contrast to DeDe Pierce's version, an elegantly poised rendition of "The Peanut Vendor." It was sublime.

Perhaps the crowning moment in my memory of Jack Willis is the night he played on the same stage as Bobby Hackett. It was during the early seventies, the occasion a traditional jazz concert at the Fairmont Hotel, as part of the New Orleans Jazz and Heritage Festival. How those days are missed! Hackett was booked to play with the Papa French band, which, besides Albert French on the banjo, consisted of Jack Willis (cornet), "Brother Cornbread" Thomas (clarinet), Homer Eugene (trombone), Jeanette Kimball (piano), Frank Fields (string bass), and returning to the band for this concert only, Louis Barbarin (drums).

The concert began cordially enough, for this was not a loud band, but a musical and swinging group that evidently suited Hackett well. Always the gentleman, Hackett quickly noticed a kindred spirit in Willis and began inviting him to play more solos. As the evening wore on, their admiration for each other became obvious to everyone in the audience as Hackett began to sound more and more like Willis, and Willis began to sound more and more like Hackett. Trading choruses on many of the tunes, their competition and imitation of each other was friendly and refreshingly non-egotistical. On one number, I think it was "Royal Garden Blues," Willis, for the most part a middle-register man like Hackett, took a phrase of his solo up to high C and down again. Hackett repeated this device with an original phrase of his own. They continued trading choruses, Willis this time ascending to high D in the middle of a phrase. Hackett smiled and once again matched Willis in range and inventiveness. Willis nodded in Hackett's direction and, as an integral part of his improvisation, rose to a high E above high C. This must have been one of the few times anyone has heard Hackett use the high register, which he did with aplomb, reaching for and playing right through the high E with grace and beauty. There was tumultuous applause as Hackett took Willis's hand for their bow together. The only glitch in the evening occurred when the MC came out at the end of the concert and announced Bobby Hackett, omitting any mention of the band. I can only think he had missed most of the performance and had no notion of how the concert had developed. It was so embarrassing to all present that the applause was a bit hesitant. Hackett saved the day by grabbing the mic, adding with a broad smile across his face: ". . . and what a wonderful band!" All the musicians deserved a share of the credit.

Shortly thereafter, Jack suffered Bell's palsy in the left side of his face, which put him into retirement for a while. His recovery was partial, and when he returned to work a couple of years later he had lost the bright edge to his tone and never regained his range. But his inventiveness, now in the low and middle range of the cornet, was undiminished. Jack continued to be held in the highest regard by other musicians, and I recall several private functions during my stint with the Papa French band in the mid-seventies when he was hired to play second cornet. Needless to say, sitting next to Jack, who could improvise a second part as easily as falling off a log, was like attending a master class. On one occasion during the time when Dave Bartholomew was normally on second trumpet, Jack was hired to play third. I suspect Bartholomew was responsible for this, for nobody enjoyed listening to Jack more that day than Dave. Jack was a musician's musician through and through, yet I have to admit that it took several years for Jack Willis's cornet playing to grow on me. Most often heard from the mid-sixties through the early seventies with Papa French's Original Tuxedo Jazz Band, Jack played in a legato style more flowing and florid than that of anyone else in New Orleans. At first I thought his lead was too busy for the band, but Jack was so capable of improvisation that I now know he was frequently holding himself back. What he played, the ideas that came to him, depended on the harmonic style of the piano player. While Jack was comfortable with a wide spectrum of music, there is no doubt that swinging on a New Orleans two-beat was second-nature to him.

Born in Illinois in 1920, Jack Willis moved with his family to an Uptown district of New Orleans around 1929. He began playing music at school and was gifted enough to begin working as a musician at the age of fifteen. His first break came when he joined Joe Robichaux's New Orleans Rhythm Boys, by now a thirteen-piece big band, which included Waldren "Frog" Joseph on the trombone, a musical friendship and partnership that was to last the rest of Jack's life.

When Robichaux let the band go, a small group of Robichaux's sidemen called The Gentlemen of Rhythm continued to work together as a cooperative group, although eventually as Frog told me, "we made Freddie Kohlman the leader." This was a New Orleans Swing band that played all the popular tunes of the day, frequently using Jack Willis's arrangements, which he would write out from piano scores. As the demand for traditional jazz increased after the war, Jack wrote out parts for the horns on these standards as well. Many younger New Orleans musicians learned from hearing the semi-arranged way Frog and Jack played this repertoire.

Along with many other New Orleans musicians, Jack Willis took up work in the rhythm 'n' blues field, a music he loved as much as any other. 1955 saw Jack playing with Ray Charles. They recorded four sides in New York for Atlantic which included Jack's arrangement of "Mary Ann," and the horn parts for "Hallelujah, Here I Come."

The Gentlemen of Rhythm front-line of Frog Joseph, Jack Willis, and Sam Dutrey was reunited in 1961 when pianist Dave "Fat Man" Williams hired them to play with him and singer Blanche Thomas at Leroy's on Bourbon Street. According to Dave Williams, it was a time when there was little work for musicians and, besides, blacks were not welcome in tourist areas. In spite of that, Dixieland Hall opened in 1962, providing a venue where these musicians could be heard throughout the sixties.

Jack Willis eventually returned to regular work with Placide Adams's Original Dixieland Hall Jazz Band which played the Sunday brunch at the Hilton Hotel. On Jack's last Sunday, October 1, 1989, so the story goes, with none other than Billy Graham in the audience, he picked up an unusual number of spirituals and hymns, enjoying himself immensely playing this simple repertoire in his usual modest way. Normally a very retiring, some would say shy person, Jack went out of his way to talk to people on the band breaks and even gave Billy Graham a hug. That evening at home, complaining of chest pains and thinking he had indigestion, he went out to get something at the corner store. On the way there and back he stopped and talked to all his neighbors. This was so out of character for Jack that everyone remarked on it, according to both Placide Adams and his wife, Lillian. While resting on a couch he thought he heard someone calling his name. "Is that you?" he asked Lillian who was in the next room. It was not. This happened several times, she said. Jack passed away later that evening.

A TALE OF JEANETTE KIMBALL

Of all the piano players I have worked with, the most engaging and rhythmic was the lady who played with Papa French's band. Previous to the time when I joined the band, the rhythm team of Jeanette, Frank Fields on string bass, and Louis Barbarin on the drums was second to none. They simply knew exactly how to send a band with a swinging two-beat and subtle syncopations that lifted the whole ensemble. And when the moment was right, they could crank it up yet another notch.

Jeanette's repertoire and musical philosophy reflected the ability of New Orleans music to absorb influences and styles from seemingly any direction. As she says, "I played any type of music; I didn't want to copy any particular style. I just like music. It was a part of me and it was my talent." Yet her piano playing had a wonderful swing and an instantly recognizable syncopated two-beat.

Jeanette Kimball (née Salvant) was born and reared in Pass Christian, Mississippi, a resort town on the Gulf Coast. She began piano lessons at age seven and was so gifted that she was actually teaching

Jeanette Kimball and Herb Hall, 1980.
Photo: Judy Cooper, courtesy of New Orleans Records.

piano when she was eleven, and played her first road show from New York at age fourteen. She credits her teacher, Mrs. Anna Stewart, a graduate of the New England Conservatory, with everything. So it was hardly surprising that when Papa Celestin needed a new pianist in 1926, he and his alto saxophone player Paul Barnes drove out to Pass Christian to audition her. "Why, Papa," declared Barnes, "I believe she can play better than us!" She was old enough to move to New Orleans, staying with her aunt.

Some of Jeanette's fondest memories are of the years spent with Celestin, who regularly commissioned arrangements, playing mostly for "society" events and dances. She left the band in 1935 to teach piano and rear her two daughters, but returned to professional music in 1946 by joining Buddy Charles's band at the Dew Drop Inn. They played behind many different acts and guest artists, typically Kansas City bluesman Wynonie Harris. She was persuaded by Papa Celestin to rejoin his band to play at the White House for President Eisenhower's inauguration.

Jeanette played the piano with a strongly accented and syncopated two-beat. Although this bore some resemblance to other New Orleans and Gulf Coast pianists, none had perfected this tantalizing rhythmic approach in quite the same way.

Jeanette became a friend, and I drove her home after the gigs on many occasions. She never revealed her age, but when she retired to live with one of her daughters in South Carolina, they told me she was born in 1906.

She and Narvin Kimball had met while playing with Papa Celestin in the late 1920s, but after their marriage broke up in the early 1950s, she went through a hard time emotionally. "I was staying with my aunt who lived in New Orleans. Then Narvin began all that foolishness," is how she described the courtship. "But when he left me, an old childhood sweetheart of mine heard about it. He called me up and said he was driving down from Atlanta to see me. I was so excited. But you know what happened? On the way down he was killed in an automobile accident. I was so depressed—for a long, long time.

"But Albert Walters—he was playing trumpet in the band—*he* cheered me up. You know—he's the one got me out of it. He was always cracking jokes and telling stories. One day I laughed so hard and it was over."

THE JAZZ LIFE

Every tub on its own bottom.

My musical activities had begun to diversify even before I left the Papa French band. Cornetist Johnny Wiggs was taking an interest in me and, as his age was catching up with him, would hire me to play second trumpet on his occasional gigs to lighten the load. We alternated responsibilities, playing lead and second. As a result of this friendship, Johnny sent me in his place whenever he felt unwell. That is how I came to play at the Manassas Jazz Festival one year, playing alongside such great musicians as Kenny Davern, Bob Wilber, Dill Jones, Maxine Sullivan, and many others.

With tourism steadily increasing throughout the 1970s, there was a time when Bourbon Street featured as many as seven clubs with traditional jazz, some with two or three bands a day. Although I was not working on a regular basis, trumpet players like Teddy Riley, Murphy Campo, Jimmy Ille, and George Finola knew I was available, and whenever they needed a night off either from sickness or from taking another gig, would call me to replace them. There was one week when I played seven gigs on Bourbon Street, each night in a different club. I was able to build stamina and strength, not only physical endurance but the persistence to repeat the most popular tunes for the tourists and make them sound fresh every time. Playing jazz in that environment was never easy or natural. I had to put out as much energy as I could muster and do my best to fit in with a variety of bands.

Yet not everything was drudgery. I loved the occasional times I played in trios or quartets for private parties, which were always creative and relaxing. One day in the late 1970s I received a call from the manager of a private club who asked me to bring in a trio for one of their tea dances—and would I please get Danny Barker on banjo? Of course I did, and we were so popular that we worked together regularly for several years. Frank Fields played the string bass with the most consistent deep tone and sense of time of anyone I can remember.

Danny's tempos were pure old New Orleans, quite the opposite of the Bourbon Street style. We played everything as a "businessman's bounce," a typical New Orleans tempo I had not heard much since the days when I first arrived in the city. Our audiences danced to every tune, after all. One time, playing for a crawfish boil for the employees of a local hospital, an African American nurse got up to dance a solo. We were playing "Tin Roof Blues" at the time and, moving every part of her body at once, her dance was sensual and yet completely natural. Everyone gathered around in a circle to watch, which reminded me of the drawing from the nineteenth century of a dancer in *Place Congo*. Our music changed immediately, tightening up with more intensity, more depth of feeling, unlike anything I had heard before. The music and the dance became one. Aha! I thought. So *that's* the blues.

I shall always treasure the compliment I received that year. While playing a weekend gig at the Gazebo in the French Market with John Royen's quartet, our drummer Al Babin suddenly looked at me with a quizzical look on his face: "Heh!" he said, smiling. "You sound like a *New Orleans* trumpet player—ALMOST."

After Papa French died, the original members of his band left one by one, and Bob French hired younger, more modern-sounding musicians to replace them. Though it was a good band, the old-line Mardi Gras krewes that hired Papa every Carnival season could not get used to that. It happened that Mr. Eastman, who organized a Mardi Gras party every year called "The Saints and Sinners," spoke to Jeanette Kimball to see if he could get the old music back.

"I told Mr. Eastman to call you," she said to me one day in 1979. "You're going to hear from him. He wants the same musicians as before. You think you can get the band back together?"

"I'd love to," I said, though somewhat taken aback by the suggestion. I knew that, incredibly, all of them were out of work. Dixieland Hall had folded in the early 1970s and Preservation Hall, with its full complement of musicians, had no work for them either.

"We want you to bring the band," said Mr. Eastman a day or so later, "as long as you have Miss Jeanette on piano. You *will* have Jeanette?"

"Absolutely!"

It was quite easy to reassemble the band. But since Homer Eugene had retired after a second stroke affected his right arm, I got "Frog" Joseph to play trombone, and with Brother Cornbread on clarinet and Frank Fields on bass, we had the nucleus of the original group. We used different drummers for a while, with Andrew Hall filling in at the beginning when we started, then talked Louis Barbarin out of retirement briefly, and subsequently used Leo Quezergue, Freddie Kohlman, and Ernie Elly. I had a new name for the band, and when I ran into Kid Sheik on the street, he exclaimed excitedly: "I hear you revived the Camellia, Wooden Joe's band name." Wooden Joe Nicholas was one of Kid Sheik's idols back in the 1920s.

So here I was, a British trumpet player with a mere twelve years spent in New Orleans, leading a band of incredible, wonderful individuals, veteran musicians all—and not only that, but at *their* request. "Do you know what you're getting into?" asked a lady in a hotel catering department.

"Probably not," I said. But what did I have to lose? We were welcomed by all the calls I received to play at the society functions that I used to play with Papa French, and the New Orleans Jazz Club gave us our first job to play for their annual party that spring. We began with the same tune that Papa French always opened with—"Basin Street Blues."

I was home.

EPILOGUE

To summarize my musical career since 1979, I will add this:

The Original Camellia Jazz Band played private and convention jobs quite frequently, although the original musicians have passed on, and so the personnel has gradually changed. We made one recording with the original members in 1979 featuring "Brother Cornbread" Thomas on the clarinet; then, after he passed, we recorded with clarinetist Herb Hall in 1980. We continued to play all the Mardi Gras krewe engagements that I had once played with Papa French.

In addition, I played three tours with "Bob Greene's World of Jelly Roll Morton" between 1979 and 1982, which included Herb Hall, clarinet; Tommy Benford, drums;, Eddie Davis, banjo; and John Williams, bass. Also, with a different band, I took over the daytime spot at the Maison Bourbon for a couple of years. We landed the Sunday Brunch at the Iberville Hotel (subsequently the Westin Canal Place) in 1984, which was very popular and gave us great exposure. We kept the job for thirteen years. By this time, Trevor Richards had returned to New Orleans and had taken over the drums in the band. On a subsequent recording and European tours we hired bassist Truck Parham from Chicago, pianist Red Richards from New York, and Charlie Gabriel on the clarinet and tenor sax. Charlie is from Thibodaux, Louisiana. He moved to Detroit for many years and is currently playing in the Preservation Hall Jazz Band.

In 2001, to celebrate the centenary of Louis Armstrong's birth, I formed the New Orleans Serenaders with pianist Butch Thompson from St. Paul, Minnesota. We played festivals in New Orleans and Switzerland and recorded a couple of times for GHB Records.

There are only a few of us who remember the music that the New Orleans musicians, who we heard in the 1960s and 70s, taught us to play. Although we are able to continue playing it amid the current, somewhat amateurish, revival of traditional jazz, when *we* are gone, so will our music and our memories. The time of the traditional New Orleans style of music will be over.

I'll say no more!

"Ça c'est plein (that's a-plenty)," as they say in New Orleans.

APPENDIX A: TWO-BEAT OR FOUR-BEAT?

To be technical about it, common time, i.e., 4/4—four quarter notes per measure—is represented by "C," and "cut time" or "split time," i.e., 2/2 time—two half notes per measure—is so called because it is represented by a "C" with a vertical slash through it. As with any time signature, we can subdivide the two strong beats into any number of weak beats we like, but we are always aware of the two strong beats. In New Orleans jazz, each half note is usually divided into two quarter notes and/or four eighth notes by the soloist, etc. Under these circumstances, when the drummer plays two beats to the bar on the bass drum, he is playing "two-beat," and when four beats to the bar, "four-beat." Two-beat and four-beat are vernacular terms in jazz for 2/2 and 4/4, respectively. Interestingly, when we accent any weak beat, we are creating syncopation and the strong beats are implied. Therefore, whenever we clap on the second and fourth quarter note of a measure, we are creating two-beat (2/2). When the bass drummer in a parade accents every eighth quarter note and leaves the next downbeat tacit, his syncopation strongly implies the next downbeat. It's a beautiful thing to feel.

When I first came to New Orleans in 1964, the bands all used a variety of accents, usually in 2/2 until the out choruses, when they switched to 4/4 for the extra drive. Many of the musicians, among them George Guesnon, Paul Barnes, and Manuel Manetta (who began playing professionally in 1904), told me this is the *rule* for New Orleans jazz—it must be that way—and insisted I learn to tap my foot two to the bar if I was ever going to get anywhere. When this rule evolved, I cannot say. And so 4/4 and 2/2 are not the same thing. The New Orleans musicians who taught me showed me how to feel the difference. On top of that, I studied rudiments of music in London and music theory at the Loyola School of Music in New Orleans, and each time I was made aware of the significant difference between the two.

In old marches and in ragtime, 2/4 and 6/8 also have two strong beats. Converting a tune written in 2/4 or 6/8 to 4/4 or 2/2 is significant. That extra step of changing the time signature is required to enable a jazz musician to swing the tune.

One example of the use of 4/4 and 2/2 in jazz: I've just heard a George Lewis recording on WWOZ in which, as Lewis preferred, Lawrence Marrero *is* playing 4/4 on the banjo, yet Slow Drag Pavageau is playing 2/2 on the bass—an effective combination which produces an intriguing ambivalence. The two-beat on the bass is dominant until the out choruses, when Drag shifts into 4/4.

APPENDIX B: WHAT DOES LOUIS ARMSTRONG MEAN?

If we had to name a "Man of the Twentieth Century," Louis Armstrong would be my choice. The more I listen to his music, the more I am in awe of him, and the more incredible his achievement seems to be. His contemporaries felt the same way. The clarinetist Albert Nicholas said once that Armstrong made all the other trumpet players sound like little boys. No wonder he swept away all before him.

And yet his recordings are but little vignettes taken out of time and caught forever on wax. The bassist Truck Parham told me that when Louis caught sight of a group of friends and musicians in the audience he would really open up. What he played on these occasions went beyond anything you could imagine. Toward the end of his life, I was fortunate enough to hear Armstrong several times and played on his seventieth birthday concert, "Hello Louis!," in Los Angeles. When I heard him in New Orleans in 1965, he gave us a brief glimpse of what Truck Parham was talking about when he unexpectedly played a variation on "The Saints" so rhythmically and melodically intricate that the whole audience gasped.

Taking the raw material from the neighborhood in which he was born, even to the extent of the language and mugging of the characters he grew up with, Armstrong was able to transform through his music the sum of all those early experiences and present it on stage for the whole world to see and enjoy.

There is no denying the emotional intensity of Louis Armstrong's music; but it also takes us to a place that I sense is beyond emotions, where the music stands purely on its own terms. There is a quality in Armstrong's tone, in his swing, spontaneity, and freedom of expression that is indefinable, yet connects directly to a place deep within us. What I hear is so much joy, so much joy even in sadness, and so much joy in his art of expressing so much joy.

GLOSSARY

Because so many authors have used musical terms incorrectly, I have decided to list some common terms with their correct meaning, along with some slang terms (in italics) used by New Orleans musicians.

American someone who moved to New Orleans after the Louisiana Purchase of 1803 from elsewhere in America, usually English-speaking and of a Protestant religion.

axe musician's term for his/her instrument (what he/she goes to work with).

backbeat same as offbeat.

bad musician's term meaning extremely good or inventive, as in "Louis Armstrong is bad, real bad."

band of music the term New Orleans musicians use to describe a band.

bridge a middle, contrasting section of a tune.

broken chord notes of a chord played in succession rather than simultaneously. Arpeggio.

cadence a progression that occurs at the close of a phrase or section, giving a feeling of a temporary or permanent ending.

changes the series of chords or harmonic progression in a tune.

channel the term New Orleans musicians used for the bridge.

close harmony two or more instruments or voices playing the melody and harmony to each note of the melody exactly together in time.

Creole originally a Portuguese term for an African servant or slave. Subsequently took on many meanings: anyone of French or Spanish descent who was born in the Colonies. "Creole of Color" was a term used to denote a person of part African and French or Spanish descent, born in the Colonies, usually French-speaking and of Catholic religion. Today in New Orleans, Creole refers to a person of mixed descent whose grandparents spoke French.

cut time 2/2 meter. Some jazz musicians call this a *swinging two-beat.*

dynamics variations in the volume of a phrase or section of a piece of music.

downbeat the first beat of the first measure, or the first beat of any measure.

four-beat common time, 4/4 meter.

gig a job for a musician.

good tonation a New Orleans musician's term for playing in tune.

heterophony different musical interpretations based on the same melody played together. Term used by Bill Russell to describe the ensemble style of the George Lewis band. Also can be used to describe the group singing in a Sanctified church.

horn musician's term for any brass or woodwind instrument.

in the groove or *in the pocket* when all the band members play with an identical rhythmic feel.

inner voice a harmony line to the melody.

intonation tuning.

lick a musical phrase.

mophodite shortened form of Hermaphrodite—a musician's term that used to be employed to describe a tune that does not follow a familiar pattern.

musicianer someone who plays music. Also: *cooker*—someone who cooks.

offbeat with four quarter notes to a measure, the "offbeats" are the second and fourth beats.

phrase a relatively short portion of a melodic line that expresses a musical idea, comparable to a line or sentence in poetry.

phrasing a musician's term for the manner of playing a melody in phrases.

riff a repeated rhythmic phrase.

routine an old expression meaning playing by routine or by ear (often pronounced "air") rather than from written music.

second line originally, those who follow the parade and dance on the side make up the second line, because the parade itself of the band and the club or church members make up the first line. Today the term "second-line parade" has come to mean any parade where people dance to the music.

time tempo. Playing with "good time" means with a steady speed, not *pushing* (speeding up) or *pulling* or *dragging* (slowing down).

turnaround the cadence that brings the melody back to a starting point.

two-beat cut time, 2/2 meter.

two-four some musicians erroneously refer to cut time as 2/4. This has confused several researchers.

unison two or more instruments or voices playing exactly together in time, either at exactly the same pitch or in a different octave.

woodshedding or *'shedding* the musician's term for practicing in private.

NOTES

6. CITY OF DREAMS

1. Kimball doubled on string bass and banjo, with Albert Walters, trumpet; Jessie Charles, clarinet; Worthia "Show Boy" Thomas, trombone; "Sing" Miller, piano; and John Robichaux, drums. With so many older musicians to choose from, none of these musicians was working at either Preservation or Dixieland Hall.

Santo Pecora and Joseph "Sharkey" Bonano alternated sets at the Famous Door. Both bandleaders were key figures among the white musicians in New Orleans and both well represented on recordings during the twenties. With Sharkey were Harry Shields, clarinet; Emile Christian, trombone; Jeff Riddick, piano; "Chink Martin" Abraham Sr., string bass; and Arthur "Monk" Hazel, drums.

Clem Tervalon's band, which included his uncle Albert Burbank on clarinet and Thomas Jefferson on trumpet, played at the Paddock Lounge.

7. A DREAM COME TRUE

1. Barbara Reid, a member of the New Orleans Society for the Preservation of Traditional Jazz.

2. The Olympia Brass Band, August 30, 1964: Louis Nelson, Eddie "King" Noble, trombones; William Brown, sousaphone; Harold Dejan, alto sax and leader; Emanuel Paul, tenor sax; Kid Sheik Colar, Andrew Anderson, Sam Alcorn, and Arthur "Red" Vigne, trumpets; George Williams, snare drum; and Henry "Booker T" Glass, bass drum. This was before Milton Batiste joined the band on first trumpet. Sitting in: Clive Wilson, trumpet; Noel "Papa" Glass and "Pickle," snare drums.

3. Renamed the William Ransom Hogan Jazz Archive in 1974.

4. Besides Bageon on trumpet were Buster Moore, trombone; Chuck Fortier, tenor sax; Harold Christophe, amplified guitar; and Dave Bailey, drums.

5. *The Baby Dodds Story, as Told to Larry Gara*, rev. ed. (Baton Rouge: Louisiana State University Press, 1992), 74.

6. Kid Thomas, Ernie Cagnoletti, trumpets; Albert Burbank, clarinet; Jim Robinson, trombone; George Guesnon, banjo; Slow Drag Pavageau, bass; and Josiah "Cie" Frazier, drums.

8. REFLECTIONS

1. With Don Redman on soprano sax were Tom Whaley, piano; Hayes Alvis, string bass; Howard Hill, banjo; Joe Thomas, trumpet; Ed Burke, trombone; and Tommy Benford, drums.

2. "Beginning their work together in 1915, Sissle and Blake's first big success on Broadway was *Shuffle Along* in 1921. A synthesis of authentic ragtime and operetta, *Shuffle Along* presented the humor, music and dance of the African American, played by an all-black cast that included Florence Mills and Josephine Baker. Being one of the few musicals of the 1920s to run for more than five hundred performances, it was a triumphant restoration of black artistry to Broadway. This production of 1964 was a nostalgic return to the roots of an earlier period." From Robert Kimball and William Bolcom, *Reminiscing with Sissle and Blake* (New York: Viking, 1973).

10. A RESIDENT ENGLISHMAN

1. The first English jazz fan anyone can remember living in New Orleans was Joan Whitehead, from Lancashire. She worked for Eastman Kodak in Rochester, New York. Her first visit was at Mardi Gras 1949, the year Louis Armstrong was King Zulu, and she lived there on and off until 1953. Subsequent "resident Englishmen" were Jonathan Lane, Ken Colyer, Richard Lane, Joe Lyde, Mike Slatter, Warwick Reynolds, Tony O'Sullivan, and Hugh Watts.

2. Previously contributed by Clive Wilson and published in *The Hottest Trumpet: The Kid Howard Story*, by Brian Harvey (New Orleans: Jazzology Press, 2007), reprinted by permission.

3. When I read Jack Kerouac's *On the Road*, I was appalled at his lack of hitchhiking skills—he did everything wrong.

11. MY NEW FAMILY

1. Banjoist Julius Handy was the bandleader, along with Herbert Permillion and Andy Anderson, trumpets; Harold Dejan and Capt. John Handy, alto saxes; Jesse Charles, tenor sax; Clem Tervalon, trombone; Joe Jackson, piano; Eddie

Dawson's nephew, electric bass; and Chester Jones, drums. Joe Jackson and Capt. Handy both lived in Pass Christian, and they played together whenever they had a job on the Gulf Coast. I enjoyed hearing Dejan and Handy challenge one another musically.

2. The union minimum in the hall was ten pieces, so the band was augmented, consisting of Willie Humphrey, clarinet; Percy Humphrey and Terry Humphrey (Willie's son), trumpets; Jim Robinson, trombone; Harold Dejan, alto sax; Emanuel Paul, tenor sax; Sing Miller, piano; Al "Battleaxe" Purnell (Alton Purnell's cousin), electric guitar; Narvin Kimball, string bass; and Alvin Woods, drums. The band was capable of providing quite a variety of music; I remember Battleaxe playing some great blues guitar later in the evening.

3. Allen and Russell, interview with Bocage, January 29, 1959, in the Hogan Jazz Archive.

12. SATURDAY NIGHT

1. "Above," "below," "front o' town," and "back o' town" are typical directions in New Orleans, where upriver is Uptown and downriver is Downtown. Therefore "above" is upriver, "below" is downriver, "front" is on the river, and "back" is away from the river.

2. Led by Ernest Milton on drums, the band was Reginald Koeller, trumpet; Eddie "Bighead" Johnson, alto sax; and John "Smitty" Smith, piano. Subsequently, Koeller and Johnson began playing at the Harmony Inn with Sing Miller, piano, and Andrew Jefferson, drums.

3. The rest of the lineup was usually Leonard Ferguson, drums; Paul Crawford, trombone; Jack Bachman, cornet; Clayton "Sunshine" Duerr, guitar; and Bill Humphries, banjo. By the time I heard the band, Raymond Burke and Hank Kmen played alternate weeks, both doubling on clarinet and tenor sax. Kmen, a history professor at Tulane University, had written the ground-breaking book *Music in New Orleans: The Formative Years, 1791–1841* (Baton Rouge: Louisiana State University Press, 1966). The book he was writing when I met him was to be titled *Black Music in New Orleans 1800–1900*, but unfortunately it was not completed before his death.

4. Allen and Russell, interview with Bocage, January 29, 1959, in the Hogan Jazz Archive.

5. The Irish Channel neighborhood is so named because at one time it lay between the English and Irish Markets. The French Market is the only one that survives today.

6. Beginning his musical career with Papa Laine's bands, Tony Fougerat went on to lead his own group, the Dominoes, which included Lester Bouchon, clarinet

and sax; Charlie Christian, trombone; and Hilton "Nappy" Lamare, banjo. He toured with a show called *The Hollywood Scandals* on the Orpheum circuit for many years before settling down again in New Orleans in 1938. The most outstanding cornet players he heard in his youth were Louis Armstrong, Kid Rena, and Emmett Hardy.

7. Besides McNeil on trumpet, the band included Albert Delone, alto sax; Leroy Robinet, tenor sax; Sammy Hopkins, piano; Ernest Roubleau, guitar; and Dave Bailey, drums.

8. Kid Thomas used Emanuel Paul, tenor sax; Ernest Roubleau, amplified guitar; Charlie Hamilton, piano; Joseph Butler, bass; and Sammy Penn, drums. On occasion I saw Louis Nelson on trombone as well.

13. PLANNING MY RETURN TO BRITAIN

1. The five New Orleans musicians were Kid Sheik Colar, trumpet; Capt. John Handy, alto sax; Louis Nelson, trombone; Chester Zardis, string bass; and Sammy Penn, drums.

14. ON THE ROAD

1. The band had Sidney Desvigne and Gene Ware on trumpets; Herb Hall and "Sport" Young (Austin's brother and Lester's cousin), alto saxes; Jesse Washington, tenor sax; Louis Nelson, trombone; Al Freeman (from Columbus, Ohio), piano; Percy Sevre, banjo; Ransom Knowling, string bass and bass horn; and Louis Barbarin, drums.

2. The band was Don Albert, Arthur Derbigny, and Hiram Harding, trumpets; Herb Hall, alto sax; Louis Cottrell, tenor sax; Frank Jacquet (Illinois Jacquet's uncle), trombone; Henry Turner, bass horn; Ferdinand Dejan (Harold Dejan's cousin), banjo; Al Freeman, piano; Albert Martin, drums; and singer Sidney Hansell.

3. Jimmy Johnson, who played in Bolden's band, came in on string bass. Philander Tiller replaced Derbigny on trumpet, and James "Dink" Taylor was added on sax.

4. Herb Hall, *Olde Tyme Modern*, Sackville Records.

15. CHANGING TIMES

1. Initially, the band at Commander's Palace was Alvin Alcorn, trumpet; Louis Cottrell, clarinet; Justin Adams, guitar; and Louis Barbarin, snare drum. Later, Alcorn had two trios working: Alcorn, trumpet, Buddy Charles, guitar; Gerald

Adams, bass; and Louis Cottrell, clarinet, Justin Adams, guitar; Placide Adams, bass.

2. The musicians on this tour were Allan Jaffe, helicon; Paul Crawford, trombone; Harold Dejan, alto sax; Emanuel Paul, tenor sax; Milton Batiste and Clive Wilson, trumpets; Andrew Jefferson, snare drum; and "Booker T" Glass, bass drum. It is possible the promoter had asked for a "mixed" band, as three of us were white—but I am speculating.

16. LA DOLCE VITA

1. Beansie owned several buildings where music used to be played, including the Astoria on South Rampart Street, San Jacinto Hall in Tremé, and Vaucresson Creole Restaurant in the French Quarter.

17. A NATURAL LIVING

1. The theory of the Mexican origin of jazz is extremely weak. New Orleans musicians did play Mexican tunes, but one could equally say that jazz began in Ireland because New Orleans musicians played Irish tunes.

2. Years later, concerning "Down by the Riverside," I remembered the West African theological belief described in Herskovits's *Dahomey*, about the journey of the soul after death. The story goes that a person must cross a river to the other side but, before crossing, the passenger must first "lay their burden down," remove their worldly clothing and dress in "long, white robes," and most importantly "lay down their sword and shield" and "study war no more"—a metaphor for relinquishing all aggression, defensiveness, and judgment. Everything, in other words, that makes up the personality—a tall order.

18. PAPA FRENCH

1. Berta Wood letter to Ken Colyer, 1957, in Mike Pointon and Ray Smith, *Goin' Home: The Uncompromising Life and Music of Ken Colyer* UK: Ken Colyer Trust, 2010), 209.

INDEX

Page numbers in **bold** refer to illustrations.
Page numbers in *italics* refer to profiles.